"Think About It, Dane. We've Been Kidding Ourselves —

how long can we continue to see each other?"

"As long as we like."

She closed her eyes and her heart twisted painfully. "We can't forget about the lawsuit. It's always there."

"Kirsten, you worry too much," Dane whispered.

"Maybe because my entire future is on the line."

"Come on, let's go to dinner—"

"But we can't be seen together," Kirsten protested softly.

"We won't," he assured her, with a devilish twinkle in his eye.

"Just what do you have in mind, counselor?"

LISA JACKSON
was raised in Molalla, Oregon and now lives with her husband, Mark, and her two sons in a suburb of Portland. Lisa and her sister, Natalie Bishop, who is also a Silhouette author, live within earshot of each other and do all of their work in Natalie's basement.

Dear Reader:

Romance readers have been enthusiastic about Silhouette Special Editions for years. And that's not by accident: Special Editions were the first of their kind and continue to feature realistic stories with heightened romantic tension.

The longer stories, sophisticated style, greater sensual detail and variety that made Special Editions popular are the same elements that will make you want to read book after book.

We hope that you enjoy this Special Edition today, and will enjoy many more.

The Editors at Silhouette Books

LISA JACKSON
A Dangerous Precedent

Silhouette Special Edition
Published by Silhouette Books New York
America's Publisher of Contemporary Romance

SILHOUETTE BOOKS
300 E. 42nd St., New York, N.Y. 10017

Distributed by Pocket Books

ISBN: 0-373-09233-4

First Silhouette Books printing April, 1985

10 9 8 7 6 5 4 3 2 1

Map by Ray Lundgren

America's Publisher of Contemporary Romance

Printed in the U.S.A.

Books by Lisa Jackson

Silhouette Intimate Moments

Dark Side of the Moon #39
Gypsy Wind #79

Silhouette Special Edition

A Twist of Fate #118
The Shadow of Time #180
Tears of Pride #194
Pirate's Gold #215
A Dangerous Precedent #233

To my grandmothers,
Tati Dickey and Tati Pederson,
with love.

A special thanks to Steve Hamilton,
for his help in understanding Oregon law.

GINEVRA: The bride who, according to a well-known story, playfully hid in a trunk on her wedding day. The lid fell, burying her alive; eventually her skeleton was discovered.

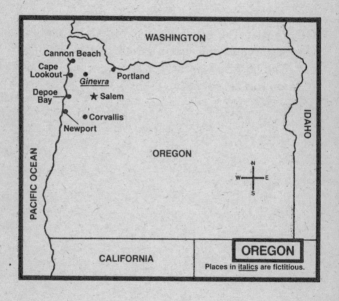

A Dangerous
Precedent

Chapter One

$\mathscr{D}$ane Ferguson hated theatrics. He was a quiet man and usually direct. Though sometimes forced by his profession to become overtly dramatic, he was never comfortable in the role and preferred the straightforward approach—the right combination of questioning and evidence to coax a witness into saying what Dane wanted the jury to hear. By nature Dane wasn't melodramatic; he expected the same of others.

Tonight he was disappointed. He had been in the room for nearly fifteen minutes, and Harmon Smith had yet to get to the point. Just how much of this theatrical demonstration was for his benefit, he wondered as he swirled his untouched drink and eyed the opulent surroundings of the president of Stateside Broadcasting Company.

Dane suspected that he had been summoned to Smith's townhouse on the Upper East Side because of the briefs he had received from that attorney in

Portland, Oregon. He had scanned the documents without much interest and passed them along to a junior associate in the firm. Now he wished he had paid more attention to the neatly typed pages.

Undoubtedly the McQueen decision was more important than Dane had originally assumed. Why else would Harmon have insisted upon this evening meeting with several of the prominent vice-presidents of SBC? Television people, Dane thought distastefully, they all love an audience.

"I think we're about ready," Harmon finally announced, motioning toward the far wall with his free hand. In the other he balanced his drink and a cigarette. A servant placed a cartridge in the video recorder.

The television seemed out of place to Dane. The twentieth-century machine was tucked between leather-bound editions in a cherrywood cabinent, and the rest of the room had been tastefully decorated in period pieces. Leather wing-back chairs, antique brass reading lamps and highly polished mahogany tables were arranged perfectly around a rare Oriental carpet of deep emerald green. There was little doubt in Dane's mind that the decorator who had created the stately effect would have preferred to exclude the tele- vision. But that was impossible. Harmon Smith lived and breathed for the tube and the six-figure income that television provided him.

Dane's deepset hazel eyes fastened on the screen, as had all the other pairs of eyes in the room. Harmon Smith wiped an accumulation of sweat from his receding hairline before taking a long swallow of his Scotch and water. The muted voices in the room quieted as an image on the screen flickered and held.

"There she is," Smith whispered through tightly

clenched teeth. He pointed a condemning finger at the woman who dominated the screen.

The object of Smith's contempt was an attractive woman who wore her smile and expensively tailored suit with ease. She descended the concrete steps with unfaltering dignity and managed to hold her poise despite the wind blowing against her face and the throng of reporters that had engulfed her.

"That's Kirsten McQueen?" Dane asked dubiously as he studied the graceful woman. His dark brows rose speculatively and a smile tugged at the corners of his mouth.

"The bitch herself," Harmon Smith answered vehemently after taking a long drag on his cigarette.

"Now, wait a minute—" Dane began to interrupt, but Smith silenced him by shaking his balding head.

"Shh . . . I want you to hear this."

"Ms. McQueen?" A pleasant-featured woman reporter with long dark hair and almond-shaped eyes accosted the graceful cause of the commotion. "We know about the decision against KPSC. Would you care to comment on the fact that the judgment in your favor is a small victory for women's rights?"

Kirsten's even smile never wavered. Her clear green eyes looked steadily into the camera. "I doubt that the decision has anything to do with women's rights, Connie. I think mine was an individual case that was brought to an equitable conclusion." It was obvious to Dane that the slender woman with the soft brown hair and intriguing green eyes was at ease in front of a camera. There was a quiet dignity about her that was captured on the film.

The reporter persisted. "Then you don't see the decision as a vote of confidence for feminism?"

"This was a lawsuit concerning age, not sex,"

Kirsten emphasized, holding her hair in place with her free hand. Raindrops had begun to shower on the crowd.

"But feminist groups throughout the state are supporting you and what you're fighting."

"And I appreciate it," Kirsten replied with the flash of even white teeth and the hint of an evasive smile.

"The women's movement could use a new heroine," the plucky newswoman suggested.

Kirsten laughed lightly. "I hardly think I qualify," she responded. Her eyes had warmed by the compliment she apparently considered absurd.

The reporter was placated. "All right. What about the rumors that the station might appeal the decision?"

Kirsten sobered. "It's their right."

"Do you think another jury would rule in your favor, considering the outcome of this trial?"

Kirsten hesitated. "That remains to be seen," she volunteered carefully. "At this point it's only conjecture and I never like to borrow trouble." The clear green eyes had clouded.

The thin blond man with the thick moustache who had been walking next to Kirsten took charge. "That's enough questions," he insisted authoritatively. His protective position of holding lightly onto Kirsten's bent elbow suggested that he was either Kirsten's husband or attorney. Dane suspected the latter—the neatly pressed three-piece suit gave the man away.

"Who is he?" Dane demanded with a frown.

"The prosecuting attorney," Frank Boswick, Smith's assistant replied.

"Is he any good?"

"Rumored to be the best Portland has to offer," Boswick allowed.

Dane's concern was evidenced in the knit of his brow and the narrowing of his eyes. "So why isn't he on our side?"

Smith waved off Dane's question with the back of his hand. "Are you kidding? Lloyd Grady has a reputation of working with the underdog. He's originally from Seattle, and apparently thought he could get some national attention through Kirsten McQueen."

The television screen darkened. Dane considered everything he had learned about Kirsten McQueen as he shifted his gaze from the television to Harmon Smith. The balding man's skin had flushed from the combination of alcohol and anger. He stubbed out his cigarette with a vengeance.

"I want to nail Kirsten McQueen," Harmon Smith spat out. His watery blue eyes lifted to meet Dane's inquisitive stare. "And I want you to do it."

"I'll consider it."

Harmon Smith's lips compressed into a thin white line. "I'm calling in all of my markers, Dane. You owe me a favor—a big one—this is it."

The amused smile that had tugged at the corners of Dane's mouth slowly disappeared and his square jaw hardened. "I said I'd consider it," he acquiesced before sitting in one of the stiff chairs. "I think you had better explain everything about this case to me—from the beginning."

"Didn't you get the information from our Portland attorney?" Smith asked. Dane's gaze sought Frank Boswick. The young assistant seemed to have a more objective approach to the case.

"The attorney in Portland is Fletcher Ross," Frank stated.

Dane took a thoughtful swallow of his brandy. "I

saw the notes, but I'd like to hear your side of the story." His dark hazel eyes had returned to Harmon Smith. Why was this case so important to him?

Smith paced nervously to the window and fumbled in his pocket for his cigarettes and lighter. He looked into the dark Manhattan night before responding. "Basically, the story is this: Kirsten McQueen is a local gal. Grew up around Portland somewhere."

"Milwaukie," Frank clarified.

"Right. Anyway, KPSC hired her right out of college." Harmon Smith blew a thick cloud of smoke at the window as he reconstructed the events that had thrown him and his corporation into the middle of this mess. "She had all the right qualifications—"

"Which were?" Dane inquired.

Smith shook his head as if it didn't matter. "You know, a degree in journalism, some work in another station, brains, interest in the news. Anyway, she worked her way up through the ranks. It was good publicity for the station to make her a full reporter because of her local connections. People eat that kind of thing up. Everybody likes to hear that a local girl made good."

Dane nodded pensively, his studious eyes never leaving Smith's worried face. Why did Kirsten Mc-Queen get under Harmon Smith's skin? She was just a small-town reporter; he was the head of a national broadcasting corporation.

"So," Harmon Smith continued, warming to his subject, "as time went by she started throwing her weight around, making ridiculous demands, becoming a real pain in the neck. Finally she was let go."

"And she sued KPSC?" Dane surmised.

"Right."

Dane thought it odd. The woman on the screen had

appeared dignified, not likely to throw her weight around. In his profession he often had to size some-one up by first impression. It helped that he had an intuitive understanding of most people's motives. In Dane's estimation, Harmon Smith must have gotten some bad information on Kirsten McQueen, or else he hadn't as yet completely leveled with Dane.

"But she didn't sue for sex-discrimination?" Dane thought aloud, conjuring a mental image of the con-servatively dressed woman with the slightly seductive smile.

"Hell, no! She wouldn't have a leg to stand on and she's smart enough to realize it. Even her replace-ment was a woman!" Harmon Smith declared.

"A younger woman," Dane guessed.

"Yeah, right," Smith grumbled. "I really don't know how old Carolyn is."

"Twenty-two," Frank supplied with an unapprecia-tive glance at his superior. "Carolyn Scott is twenty-two."

"Whatever," Smith acknowledged with a wrinkled frown. "It really doesn't matter."

"And this new woman . . . this Carolyn Scott . . . she's qualified?" Dane asked.

"Yeah, sure."

"All the right qualifications," Frank agreed.

Dane tugged on his lower lip. "I really don't understand something here," he admitted. "Kirsten McQueen doesn't look all that old to me."

"She's not!" Smith stated angrily. "My point exact-ly. That's why this whole goddamn mess is so hard to swallow!"

"How old is she?" Dane inquired evenly.

"Somewhere around thirty."

"Thirty-five," Frank corrected him. "You may as

well level with Dane, Harmon," the young assistant advised. "He's on *our* side."

"Wait a minute," Dane interjected. "How can a thirty-five-year-old woman win an age-discrimination suit?"

"Beats me," Smith allowed. "Only in Oregon. Those people out there aren't in tune with the rest of the nation. They're always on some new crusade! It's either a bottle bill, or a clean-water act, or easier laws on possession of marijuana—whatever. I even think an Oregon woman prosecuted her husband for rape, for God's sake!"

"That's right," Frank agreed. "The competition made a television movie out of it."

"Figures," Smith snorted angrily. "Now it looks like it's KPSC's turn."

Dane set his drink on the table and stood to face Harmon Smith squarely. "So you think public sentiment won the case for Kirsten McQueen?"

"It sure as hell didn't hurt it!" Smith waved angrily in the air and shrugged his shoulders as if Dane's questions were irrelevant.

"How many women does KPSC employ?" Dane's gaze shifted to Frank Boswick.

"Eleven," the young assistant replied.

"And how many are over thirty-five?"

"Two."

Dane's dark brows arched. "And neither of them is in front of the camera—right?"

Frank Boswick smiled and shook his head. "One woman who's forty does special-interest stories once a week," he stated, shooting his boss a glance that dared the older man to dispute the facts. "However, she wasn't promoted until after Kirsten McQueen filed suit."

"Great," Dane muttered, starting to see the evidence stacking against KPSC. His eyes narrowed with the challenge and he concentrated on a premise for defense. "So why are you involved, Harmon? Isn't this a problem with the station in Portland?"

"It should be," Frank agreed.

Smith let out a disgusted sigh. "The reason Stateside Broadcasting Company is involved is because we own a percentage of our affiliated stations. Granted, that percentage is small, but we're still involved."

"And that includes KPSC," Dane surmised.

"Right." Harmon Smith thought Dane was finally becoming interested in the case. "And Kirsten McQueen's decision is dynamite. Not only will it affect our other affiliates throughout the country, it could have ramifications for the entire industry."

"A dangerous precedent?" Dane asked.

"Exactly." Smith refilled his drink from a well-stocked bar. "That clip you saw is three months old. We've appealed the decision and the State Court of Appeals in Oregon has ordered a new trial; the date is set for early October, I think. I want you to represent KPSC. You can work with the Oregon attorney for the station."

Dane eyed Smith warily. "How involved will I be?"

"You'll call the shots."

"That will be difficult from New York."

Smith's eyes turned cold. "Then you'll have to go to Oregon."

Dane was reluctant. "I don't know if I can spare the time. I've got several cases scheduled for trial this summer here, in New York."

Smith pursed his lips. "Can't some associate handle them?"

"One of the partners . . . maybe, but you can't

expect me to spend all my time working on this one case across the country in Oregon."

"I don't give a damn how much time you spend out there. I just want to win and end all of this. And I expect you to keep it quiet. We don't need any more publicity." Harmon Smith's icy blue eyes narrowed with suppressed rage. "Don't worry about your fee. I don't care how much this case costs, I just want to be certain that we overturn that McQueen decision once and for all."

"That might be difficult."

"That's why I want you!"

Kirsten ran her fingers over the rim of the plastic insert of her coffee cup. She twirled it in her hands while she waited for Lloyd. What was taking him so long? The building was unseasonably warm and Kirsten was nervous. She never felt completely at ease talking with lawyers, even her own. And the thought of facing Fletcher Ross again turned her stomach.

Maybe she was foolish to continue her battle against the television station; maybe she should give up. They seemed to have inexhaustible sources of money to try the case. She didn't. She stared unseeing at the watercolors adorning the walls. The seascapes she had once found fascinating didn't interest her today. Nor did the clean blond modern furniture or anything else to do with Grady and Sullivan, Attorneys-at-Law. She was wrung-out—tired of lawsuits and even wearier of smug attorneys in stiff business suits. The less she had to do with them, the better.

Lloyd entered the room and Kirsten knew at that

instant that something was wrong. His smile was tighter than normal, his brown eyes worried.

"Sorry I kept you waiting," he said as he slipped into the chair next to hers.

She returned his disturbed grin. "It's all right. What's up?"

He shifted in the chair and crossed his arms over his chest. "There's been a couple of changes in the strategy of the defense."

She arched her brows inquisitively. "Such as?"

"They've got another lawyer."

She wasn't surprised. Fletcher Ross hadn't been well prepared or convincing, even to her. "So they're replacing Ross. . . ."

"Not exactly." He looked her steadily in the eyes.

"What do you mean?"

Lloyd let out a disgusted breath of air. "They've hired someone to help Ross with the defense." His dark eyes were serious and his smile had all but disappeared.

Kirsten ignored the sense of dread his words had inspired and stiffened her spine. "Someone whom you consider a worthy opponent," she guessed.

"At the very least," Lloyd reluctantly agreed.

"You act as if the guy is F. Lee Bailey." Lloyd leaned back in his chair. "Or maybe God," Kirsten continued, trying to lighten the mood.

"Not quite," Lloyd admitted with only a hint of a smile.

"But a close second?"

"You might say that. The guy's name is Ferguson, Dane Ferguson."

Kirsten shrugged her slim shoulders. "I don't think I've ever heard of him."

"I'll bet you have—think."

Kirsten tossed the vaguely familiar name over in her mind. She couldn't identify it with any particular incident. She shook her head pensively.

"He comes from New York."

"That explains it," Kirsten joked. "KPSC never let me cover any of the national stories . . . you know, too much thinking involved for a woman."

"Look, Kirsten, this is serious," Lloyd stated.

"Of course it is."

"Ferguson's got a reputation in the East."

Kirsten's smile fell from her face. "A big gun?"

Lloyd nodded. "Yeah, I guess you could call him that. He's not as flamboyant as Bailey, but he's sharp, very sharp." Lloyd thought for a moment. "He usually handles corporate cases—mergers, takeover bids, that sort of thing."

"Then why does he want to bother with me? What's a hotshot New Yorker doing out here?" The absurdity of the situation did not amuse Lloyd Grady. Not at all.

"From what I understand, he's been hired by SBC to turn this case around."

"Why? What does Stateside Broadcasting Company care about this?" Kirsten asked, feeling suddenly very small.

"I looked into it. They own part of KPSC."

Kirsten was incredulous. Her green eyes widened in amazement. "And so they want to spend a lot of money on this case. It doesn't make any sense, Lloyd. They'll probably pay this Ferguson character more than the two hundred thousand the jury awarded me."

"I don't think this was a purely economic decision," Lloyd stated, pinching his lower lip.

"It's not the money?" Kirsten was dubious.

Lloyd shook his head. "I don't think so. It's the principle of the thing that bothers Stateside. They want to make an example of you to all their affiliates."

"Dear God." Kirsten sighed. "Can't they leave me alone?"

"That's precisely what they're asking themselves about you," Lloyd surmised. "The way they see it, you're the one rocking the boat."

Kirsten raised her hand to her forehead and gently rubbed her temples. The headache that had been threatening all morning had begun to pound behind her eyes. "So what are you suggesting, Lloyd," she whispered, "that we throw in the towel?"

"Not yet." Lloyd drummed his fingers on the table. "Let's wait them out and see what Ferguson's strategy is. He's flying in tomorrow to take your deposition."

"Tomorrow!" Her eyes met Lloyd's. "Good Lord!"

"Don't worry."

"Don't worry?" she echoed, astonished. "You just told me that Dane Ferguson is one of the most prestigious lawyers in New York City and now you ask me not to worry?"

"I just wanted you to know what to expect."

"But I already gave my deposition."

"Apparently Ferguson wants to do the questioning."

"Great," Kirsten murmured sarcastically.

"You can handle it," Lloyd predicted with more confidence than he felt. "It doesn't matter who defends the case. I still think it's solidly in your favor."

"Then why the scare tactics?"

"I want you to be ready for Ferguson. He's slick. Don't let him con you into saying anything you don't mean."

"You act as if that might be easier said than done."

"Just remember that you're in the right," Lloyd advised.

"Let's just hope you can convince the jury of that." Lloyd smiled resignedly. "We did once before."

"And look where it got us."

"Come on, Kirsten, we're not defeated yet. Don't be so pessimistic. Where's your spirit? Think of the challenge of it all!"

A spark of life lighted her eyes. "I suppose you're right," she conceded with a wan smile. "It's just that I'm getting tired of all this legal nonsense. I don't know if it will ever end."

"The wheels of justice turn slowly," Lloyd kidded her. "Think of it as fun," he suggested, but his face remained grim.

"Fun?" Kirsten repeated. "If you think this is going to be fun, I'd hate to see what you do for a good time."

He cocked his head. "What if I offered to show you?" he asked suddenly.

"I'd say forget it. We have too much work to do," she countered with a convincing toss of her head. Long ago she had learned how to deal with forward men, and she knew that Lloyd had harbored more than a casual interest in her for the past several weeks. He was a reasonable man. After a few pointed rebuffs he would get the message.

"All right, but the least you can do is have dinner with me."

"With what you charge per hour," she teased, "no way."

"Be serious."

Her eyes turned suddenly cold. "I am, Lloyd. And I'm not in the market for a man. You should know that as well as anyone."

All too well he remembered the details of her divorce. "It was only a suggestion."

Kirsten nodded. "I know—why don't we wait until the case is tried? Maybe we can have a victory celebration." She hoped to spare his feelings while inwardly acknowledging that the chances for dinner with him were slim. She just wasn't interested in Lloyd Grady, or any man for that matter. What she needed was a job. She hoped the position she had applied for in San Francisco would work out.

"Okay," Lloyd agreed. "You're on. Now, about Ferguson. Can you be here tomorrow afternoon?"

"To meet with him?"

"To be grilled by him," Lloyd corrected her.

Kirsten's features tightened. "I wouldn't miss it for the world."

Chapter Two

$\mathcal{D}$ane decided that Fletcher Ross was a second-rate attorney at best. As he watched the husky lawyer he came to the conclusion that Fletcher Ross was hiding something. Dane studied all of Ross's exaggerated movements while listening to the Portland lawyer's remarks concerning the McQueen decision.

Ross puffed importantly on a cigar and paced near the window as he described in detail all of the shortcomings of the original trial. The wily man had more excuses than New York had taxicabs— everything from surprise witnesses to the baffling change of trial dates, and that didn't begin to include the fact that the jury was preponderantly unbalanced, composed of two women to every man. In Ross's inflated estimation, he didn't have a prayer going into the courtroom, and he was trying desperately to convince Dane of the same.

He failed. Dane Ferguson had too many years of

courtroom experience and he knew just how frail Fletcher Ross's excuses were. After hearing for the third time about how Ms. McQueen had conned the jury, Dane looked pointedly at his watch. It was a gesture that Ross didn't miss. He cut short his long-winded explanation.

"I suppose we should head over to Grady's office," the hefty lawyer suggested. "My car is in the lot."

"Let's walk," Dane replied with authority. "I could use some fresh air."

"It's nearly ten blocks—" Ross began to argue, but thought better of it when he noticed the surprise in Ferguson's eyes. Obviously the New Yorker was used to having his commands obeyed. The last thing Ross could afford was to offend Dane Ferguson or anyone remotely associated with KPSC. He should have won that McQueen case, and the look in Dane Ferguson's dark eyes accused him of that fact. Ross managed a well-practiced smile. "Sure, why not walk? It's a great day." He gathered his correspondence and notes before pushing them carelessly into his briefcase.

Dane rose from his chair and handed Ross's copies of the depositions taken earlier back to the Portland attorney.

"I hope they were helpful," Ross offered, accepting the documents and snapping his case shut.

Dane nodded absently. "Some of them . . . but I have a few more questions for Ms. McQueen and I want to *see* her reaction to them."

"Good luck," Fletcher Ross muttered as he opened the door to his office and held it for his New York colleague.

"Will I need it?" Dane inquired.

Ross cocked his head. "It wouldn't hurt," he conceded, stepping into the bright sunlight. Secretly he hoped that Dane Ferguson would put the screws to Kirsten McQueen—she deserved it. Losing that case had placed an irrevocable black mark on Ross's career.

Dane had to squint against the brilliance of the sunshine reflected by the minute particles of glass in the concrete sidewalk. At the intersections, where part of the concrete had been replaced by brick, the reflection wasn't so hard on his eyes. "I thought it always rained out here," he remarked, remembering the image of Kirsten McQueen talking to reporters against a darkened sky.

"It usually does," Ross responded breathlessly. He had to walk briskly to keep up with Dane's longer strides. "I guess we're having an early summer."

The offices of Grady and Sullivan were situated on the twentieth floor of a red brick tower located one block away from the Willamette River. This was the heart of the city, the business district of Portland, and the rent was considerably higher than that of the office Fletcher Ross occupied near Old Town. It made him uncomfortable and served to remind him of all his shortcomings.

During the elevator ride Dane was silent, immersed in private thoughts of how he was going to question Kirsten McQueen. From what he had read of her, and his own impression from the film clip, he knew that his job wasn't going to be easy. He smiled at the thought. He always had enjoyed a challenge, and Ms. McQueen was certain to be that and more.

At precisely two-thirty the secretary called Lloyd on the intercom. "Mr. Ross and Mr. Ferguson are here," she announced without any trace of inflection.

"Good. I'll bring Ms. McQueen and meet them in the boardroom." Lloyd turned his attention away from the intercom to focus on Kirsten. "We're on," he stated, rising from the desk. "Just remember to remain calm and answer any of Ferguson's questions directly. If you don't understand a question, ask him to rephrase it. If you get into trouble, let me know— I'll try to get you out of it. Remember: We're not on trial."

"Not today," she replied, straightening her jacket and walking with Lloyd to the door.

"Any other questions?" he asked. When she shook her head he touched her lightly on the shoulder. "This will be easier than you expect," Lloyd promised.

"It has to be," she replied wryly, "because I expect it to be the worst couple of hours of my life."

"You're kidding. . . ." It sounded like a question.

"A little."

"You'll do great," the attorney said, holding the door for her before leading her to the reception area. A young girl with doe eyes and straight blond hair turned from her typewriter as they approached.

"Mr. Ross and Mr. Ferguson are in the boardroom. I already gave them coffee."

"Good."

Lloyd pushed open the door to the boardroom. Sitting on the far side of the long oak table were Kirsten's opponents. They looked up as she walked into the room. Ross slid a disdainful glance down her body, but the other man, the one who had to be Ferguson, held her gaze boldly as he straightened from his chair to acknowledge her presence. Kirsten swallowed back the sudden dryness in her throat and managed to hold Dane Ferguson's uncompromising stare. His eyes were hazel and suspicious, his chin strong and jutted, his physique lean, but broad-shouldered. He looked as if he knew exactly what she was thinking.

Fletcher Ross was making introductions. Kirsten nodded politely on cue, managed to accept Dane Ferguson's brief handshake, and then gratefully sank into a chair opposite him. In a corner of the room, wedged between the bookcase and her machine, sat the court reporter. She was in position and ready to record every word of the conversation for future use in the courtroom.

Kirsten had been through this procedure before the original trial. At that time she had felt violated, strong and ready for a challenge. There was no doubt that she could meet the opposition head-on. But today she felt uncharacteristically weak, like a caged animal trapped behind imprisoning bars. She attempted to hide her frailty behind a cool façade of poise, the same poise she assumed when she was in front of the camera.

Lloyd cast her a reassuring glance as the questions began. It was Dane who spoke.

"All right, Ms. McQueen, I'm going to ask you a few simple questions." He ignored the skeptical rise of one of her finely arched brows. "I want you to answer them honestly and if you don't understand a question, I expect you to tell me so." He paused and his hazel eyes drove into hers. She sensed a danger in their vivid depths. This man's one intent was to discredit her. He would attempt to trap her—entice her into saying anything that might destroy her credibility. He wanted to prove that she was nothing more than a greedy liar bearing a grudge against KPSC. He was still waiting for her response.

Slowly she nodded her head.

"You'll have to speak," he reminded her pointedly. "The stenographer can't record head movements."

Her green eyes were a study in indifference. "I realize that, Mr. Ferguson."

"Good. Then if you're ready, we'll get to it. Your name is Kirsten McQueen?"

"Yes." Her expression told him how ridiculous the preliminary questions were. He ignored the disdain in her eyes.

"How old are you?"

"Thirty-five."

"And how long did you work for KPSC?" He eyed her steadily. Though his voice remained toneless, she could feel the intensity of his words.

"Nine years and eight months."

His eyes darted to his notes. "I thought you were hired directly out of college."

"I was."

Dane Ferguson smiled familiarly and Kirsten was instantly wary. He folded his arms over the tabletop and studied every small detail of her face, realizing uncomfortably that hers was a disturbingly under-stated beauty that could melt the hearts of a jury. "That doesn't add up, Ms. McQueen."

Kirsten froze. There was something in the cajoling smile and coaxing eyes flecked with gold that made her muscles tense. "Pardon me?"

"Just how long did it take you to finish college?"

She felt an old anger beginning to surface, but she managed to hold it at bay. "Less than four years."

He looked genuinely puzzled. "How then do you account for the time discrepancy?"

She surveyed him coolly. Lloyd nodded, en-couraging her to let go of a few personal facts. "I worked between high school and college at KRCT radio."

"To put yourself through school?"

"Yes." She bit out the answer as if he were getting too close to her. She was beginning to feel uncomfortable; the questions were getting much too personal, reminding her of a time she would rather forget.

Dane hesitated a moment. He was beginning to rattle Kirsten McQueen. Though she tried to hide it, he could see the quiet anger resting just beneath the surface of her intriguing green eyes. She began to play with her coffee cup, and then as if she suddenly realized her actions were a display of weakness, she folded her hands in her lap. He closed in.

"Did you help put your husband through college?"

For a moment her voice failed her. "Yes," she finally whispered.

"You were divorced . . . when was it? Two years ago?"

"Four. It was four years ago this month." She had to clear her throat.

"Why did you divorce him?" The question hung stagnantly on the air. Anger colored her cheeks and her delicate jaw tightened.

"I don't see that this has anything to do with—"

"Why did you divorce him?" Dane repeated a little more loudly. Lloyd motioned with his hands for Kirsten to calm down.

"It . . . it didn't work out," she replied lamely.

"Why?"

Kirsten bristled. Her eyes narrowed. "My husband was having an affair, Mr. Ferguson. He couldn't seem to make a choice between me and . . . this other woman."

"So you divorced him?" Was there disdain in his cold dark eyes?

There were so many other factors involved in the divorce. How could she begin to explain to this stranger the hurt and the hours of torment she had endured because of Kent? Even if she could tell him about it, he would only use it against her in the courtroom. "Essentially, yes," she replied.

Dane had hit a sensitive nerve. It was apparent in the flush on Kirsten's skin and the deadly gleam in her eyes. She was daring him to proceed with this line of questioning, but he had no choice. Empathy didn't enter into the case. The truth did.

"The woman with whom your husband was having this affair—was she younger than you?"

Every muscle in Kirsten's body was beginning to ache with the tension taking hold of her. She felt an accumulation of sweat between her shoulder blades. "Yes," she admitted, her chin rising just a fraction of an inch.

"Much younger?"

"Twelve years."

"I see," he commented dryly. It was obvious from the emotionless expression on his face that he didn't see—not at all.

He quickly scanned his notes and pretended interest in them. "And the woman who replaced you at KPSC is also younger than you, isn't she?"

"Yes." Kirsten drew in a long breath. She understood Dane's line of thinking. Thought it was ridiculous, it bothered her.

"By how many years?"

"I'm not sure—about thirteen, I think." An angry tide of scarlet crept up her neck. "Look, Mr. Ferguson, if you're insinuating—" Lloyd raised his palm, reminding her of the danger of straying from short, succinct responses to Dane Ferguson's questions.

Dane was interested. "What do you think I was insinuating?"

"Nothing," she replied in a vengeful whisper. "Let's get on with it."

"All right, Ms. McQueen. Now, tell me. Why do you think you were discriminated against—what was the reason—age? You're hardly what I would consider ready to be put out to pasture."

He was leading her, putting on a little of the country-boy charm through his light eastern accent. Kirsten didn't buy his ploy for a minute.

"What, exactly, is your question?"

He smiled. It was a genuine smile that slowly spread over his rugged features, and it let her know that he appreciated her perception. *My God,* she thought to herself, *he thinks I'm a challenge!* She had to remind herself that his smile was deadly. "Tell me why you think you were discriminated against."

"Isn't that all written out in the court documents?"

"I want to hear your side," he countered. "Humor me."

From the corner of her eye she saw Lloyd nod. She looked Dane Ferguson squarely in the eye, mustering all the conviction she had felt on the day she was let go. "They fired me because they thought I was too old to be in front of the camera."

"At thirty-five?" He was dubious.

"Yes!"

"Does the station have a written policy about such matters?"

"I don't think so."

"Then why do you think you were too old?"

An amused smile tugged at the corners of Kirsten's full lips. "I didn't think I was too old, the station did."

Dane settled back in his chair. "I find that hard to believe." It wasn't a question and she didn't respond, refusing to be baited. "If KPSC doesn't have a written policy, how did you come to the conclusion that you were discriminated against? Many people are let go and replaced by younger, less expensive employees."

"No woman at KPSC is in front of the camera after she turns thirty-five," Kirsten stated, immediately regretting her words when she noticed the widening of his boyish grin. Damn it, she'd let him goad her into saying something she shouldn't have.

"So this is sex—not age—discrimination."

Lloyd interrupted. "This is an age-discrimination suit," he reaffirmed.

Dane was attempting to lure Kirsten into dangerous territory and she had to fight the urge to tell him where to get off. "Very few older men are allowed under the lights," she added, amending her earlier statement.

The New Yorker again surveyed his notes. "But KPSC does employ one woman near forty for on-camera work—and there's a gentleman, Ted Sharp, who's been with the station for nearly ten years as the weatherman. He's forty-seven." Dane's eyes drove deeply into hers. "Certainly you can see my problem in understanding your case," he stated calmly, imploring her without words to enlighten him. He rested his square chin in his hand and waited patiently for her response.

Kirsten swallowed back the hot, infuriated words she felt forming on her tongue. She wanted to tell him how she loathed what he was doing to her, how her past was none of his business, but she didn't. She felt her fingernails digging into her thighs, carefully hiding her tension beneath the edge of the table. Forcing a smile to her lips, she faced her attacker and remained quiet, letting the waiting game continue. She braced herself against another onslaught of questions, evidence to be used in the unending assault against her character. It took all of her concentration to hide her true feelings.

"Did you have any other problems at KPSC?" Dane asked, suddenly lifting his eyes from his notes.

Kirsten shifted uneasily in her chair. Just how much did Dane Ferguson know? How much more could he guess? His eyes were unreadable, his jutted chin unforgiving. She guessed him to be a loner, a solitary man living in the city. "What do you mean?"

"For the most part, Ms. McQueen, your employee records are impeccable." Was he kidding? Kirsten suspected that Aaron Becker had crucified her once she was gone. "But there is some mention about your dissatisfaction with your job."

"Some mention?" Kirsten repeated, incredulous. "You mean a memo from the station manager, Aaron Becker? Was that dated before or after I was let go?" she inquired with just the trace of sarcasm. Lloyd stiffened and shot her a warning glance.

Dane's eyebrows rose fractionally as he watched Kirsten brush back a strand of her light brown hair. "Were you dissatisfied?"

"Not really—"

"What does that mean?" he prodded, knowing he was on the verge of discovering her weakness. Lloyd Grady shook his head slightly. It was intended for Kirsten, but Dane saw it.

"I mean that I was as satisfied as the next person."

Dane was onto something. He could see it in the

nervous glances passing between lawyer and client. The personnel records for the station lay in front of them, and he sensed that within the thick folder was the key to the puzzle. Why couldn't he see it? Just what the devil was Kirsten McQueen trying to hide? The woman and the mystery piqued his interest. Something was definitely bothering Ms. McQueen, and Dane doubted that it had much to do with age discrimination.

"Your employee records indicate that you continually demanded more challenging work. You asked to cover more diversified stories." His gold-flecked eyes rose questioningly. He searched her face for a clue.

"That's true," she admitted hastily, her palms beginning to sweat.

"Then you weren't satisfied with your work?" That same damned question.

"Not completely, no."

"Your job lacked challenge?" Dane was obviously surprised. "But you were a newscaster. That in itself is quite an accomplishment, and, I would think, a challenge." Kirsten remained silent. "Ms. McQueen," Dane said, leaning forward and pushing his angular face closer to hers, "didn't you enjoy your job at KPSC?"

"Yes."

"I want you to level with me. Something isn't right here." He pointed to the employee records with one long finger. "Something between you and KPSC. Now, I can't do my job until I understand what it is that's bothering you—and you can't expect a jury to come to an equitable decision if you withhold evidence."

"Is that what you're trying to achieve, an equitable decision?" she asked dubiously.

"Of course."

Fletcher Ross looked as if he were finally going to make a comment, but he decided against it and nervously turned his attention to the window of the large room. He pretended interest in the view of Mt. Hood while he fidgeted with the hem of his sleeve. Anxious beads of perspiration began to dot his wrinkled brow.

Lloyd intervened on Kirsten's behalf. "I don't think this is the time or the place to accuse my client of withholding evidence. If you don't have any more questions"—his gaze included both attorneys on the opposite side of the polished table—"then let's end this thing and all go home."

The New York lawyer was frustrated. He anxiously rubbed the knuckle of his forefinger with his thumb. "I'll agree to that, Lloyd, if you can assure me that Ms. McQueen will agree to another deposition should I need any further information." His response was directed to Lloyd, but his eyes never left Kirsten's face.

Lloyd's brow puckered. "I don't think that will be necessary. You've asked enough questions today, and you have all the testimony from the first trial—"

"It's all right, Lloyd," Kirsten interjected, glad for any excuse to be done with the interview. She rose from the table to her full height and managed to rain her most disarming smile on Dane Ferguson. "Anytime Mr. Ferguson wants to ask me more questions, I'll be glad to answer them."

Dane was suspicious of Kirsten's motives, but he hid his skepticism by standing and taking her outstretched palm, shaking it briefly. He had to hand it to her; she had guts—and class. An enticing mystery was Kirsten McQueen—daring one moment, vulnerable the next. Dane had trouble understanding her, and that bothered him—a lot.

"Thank you for your time," Dane stated as he released her hand.

"My pleasure." The words sounded sincere, but there was a coldness in her gaze that detracted from her polite sophistication. "If you'll excuse me," she requested with a stiff smile. When no one objected, she picked up her purse, turned on her high heel and left the boardroom.

Thank God, Kirsten thought to herself. *Thank God it's over. I hope I don't have to face Ferguson again until the trial!*

Chapter Three

𝒟ane was left with an uneasy feeling in the pit of his stomach and the sour taste of deception in his throat. Something wasn't right about this McQueen case, and he didn't know exactly what it was. That fact alone irked him.

As he paced impatiently in his hotel room, he slid a glance at his copy of all the depositions taken earlier in the week. The papers were where he had left them, scattered over a small table near the bed. Not only had he deposed Kirsten McQueen, but also several of the employees of KPSC who had known and worked with her. And the statements didn't seem to go with Fletcher Ross's evaluation of the case. That wasn't surprising. What was disturbing was the fact that Dane felt something—some piece of evidence—was missing from the neatly typed documents and he couldn't for the life of him figure out what it was.

He felt the weight of an angry frustration settling

on his shoulders. He'd been up half the night reviewing the depositions and still hadn't been able to find the answer to his problem. He swore silently to himself as he walked between the bed and window of his hotel room. Alternately he studied the expensive weave of the carpet and the view of the Ross Island Bridge stretching over the silvery waters of the Willamette River.

The airline ticket for a flight back to New York weighed heavily in his pocket. He had business back in Manhattan, a pressing matter that couldn't be put off indefinitely, and yet Dane knew that he wasn't finished in Oregon. The McQueen case stuck in his craw, and he was forced to admit to himself that it wasn't just the issue that held his interest; it was the intriguing plaintiff as well. Kirsten McQueen had managed to get under his skin. The thought galled him, and he spread his fingers before raking them through his unruly dark hair. If she had managed to permeate his thick wall of indifference, there was no doubt that she would be hell on a jury. This case was going to be a lot rougher than he had hoped.

He checked his watch. It was noon in Manhattan. Dane scowled as he picked up the phone. He'd wasted too much time in Portland as it was. Within a minute he was connected with his office near Wall Street.

His secretary wasn't pleased. He could hear her disapproval in the clipped tone of her response when he explained that he might not be back in New York as early as he had planned. "What about the Taylor hearing on Tuesday?" Madeline asked.

"I'll be back for it," Dane replied thoughtfully. He couldn't afford to anger Clarise Taylor, and the hearing couldn't be delayed.

"Mrs. Taylor expects to see you Monday afternoon—"

"See if she can make it Tuesday morning—better yet, tell her I'll call her the minute I land at LaGuardia."

"She won't be pleased."

"Is she ever?" Dane asked, and the frosty tone of his secretary instantly melted.

"I suppose not. I was just trying to avoid another scene."

"Impossible," Dane muttered. "Don't worry. If things go as I hope, I'll be back in town early tomorrow morning and I'll see Clarise as scheduled."

"God help you if you don't," Madeline said.

When Dane hung up the phone he wondered if he had made the right decision. What could he expect to accomplish in a few extra hours? The meeting with Fletcher Ross had reinforced Dane's assumption that the Portland attorney wasn't worth the time of day. The help Ross had offered Dane had been minimal, and there seemed to be a shadowy distrust in Ross's eyes. Whenever Fletcher Ross couldn't answer a question directly, a deep-seated resentment surfaced on his round features. At first Dane had dismissed Ross's actions as inconsequential. After all, the man had a right to feel indignant. The fact that Dane had been asked to oversee the defense of KPSC was in effect a slap in the Portland attorney's face. But now Dane suspected there was more than professional indignation in Fletcher Ross's silent wariness. It was as if the husky lawyer were covering his tracks. Why? Had Fletcher Ross blown the first trial so badly that he thought his career was on the line?

Dane knew he had to talk to Kirsten again, but he loathed the idea of another deposition. Confronting her within the crowded confines of an attorney's sterile office stuffed with opposing lawyers, disinterested secretaries and grim-faced court reporters wasn't what he desired. He felt compelled to see her alone, to study the depths of her wide eyes with no one else to disturb him. He cursed himself for his own impetuosity. Though it wasn't illegal to seek her out without counsel, it was unethical and Dane was used to doing everything strictly by the book. If he'd learned anything, it was that he would never again be coerced into talking behind closed doors.

"Don't be a fool," he uttered out loud, chastising himself as the memory of that one fatal error surfaced in his tired mind. His lips thinned as he considered the unfortunate Stone Motor Company decision and what it had cost him personally. Everything of value in his life had been savagely ripped from him—cruel punishment for the pain he had inadvertently caused others. His reasons for living had been destroyed, and he had vowed to himself that he would never make the same unconscionable mistake again. And yet, here he was, pacing in an overpriced hotel room in Portland and contemplating the unthinkable.

His square jaw hardened and his eyes narrowed speculatively when he telephoned the law offices of Grady and Sullivan. There was only one answer to his dilemma: the right one. He had to see Kirsten McQueen and her attorney. And then he had to shake her story.

It was a full five minutes before Dane managed to get through to Lloyd Grady. He could hear the restraint in the other man's voice.

"I'd like to depose Kirsten McQueen again," Dane announced after exchanging preliminary civilities with Kirsten's attorney.

"I'm sure we could arrange it."

"Is it possible this afternoon?" Dane inquired, knowing his request to be somewhat out of the ordinary.

"I'm afraid that's impossible. My afternoon is full."

"Perhaps your partner could sit in?"

"Out of the question," Lloyd replied smugly. This case was his baby and he wasn't about to let anyone, not even Sullivan, handle any aspect of it. Already there had been some national coverage of the McQueen decision, and if he played his cards right, Lloyd Grady could make a big name for himself.

Dane wasn't put off easily. When push came to shove, he usually got his way. "Is there another time this weekend that might work out?"

"I don't think so."

With each of Lloyd Grady's quick objections Dane's persistence grew. "I'd like to meet with Ms. McQueen before Monday because I have to be back in New York for a hearing on Tuesday."

"Then I guess you're out of luck," Lloyd responded, feeling suddenly very relieved. "Unless you want Fletcher Ross to handle the deposition."

Over my dead body, Dane thought to himself and smiled at Lloyd's obvious ploy. Too bad he was the opposition. "I don't think so."

"Well, then, you'll have to wait until you're back in town," Lloyd observed, wiping an accumulation of sweat from his nose. Dane Ferguson, or at least the man's weighty reputation, unnerved him.

"Or perhaps I can speak with Ms. McQueen myself?"

The request stunned Lloyd, but he quickly found his tongue. "I don't think so," he said hastily. "Let's keep this strictly aboveboard." There was a pause in the conversation, and Lloyd wondered if Ferguson had heard him. "I've advised Kirsten not to speak with you or any of your associates without my presence."

"And she's agreed to that?"

There was the slightest hesitation. "In essence, yes."

"Then find another time for a deposition before next Monday."

"I'm afraid that's impossible."

"This is only Thursday," Dane reminded the stubborn Portlander.

"But Ms. McQueen is out of town."

Dane smiled to himself at the small piece of information. "Can't you get hold of her? She might consider my request."

"The point is, I'm not about to ask her," Lloyd stated with renewed authority. "You had your chance, Ferguson, and I was happy to comply with your schedule. But I'm not about to inconvenience my client again, not now. If you want another deposition at a time suitable to both parties, I'll agree to it." The Portland attorney's voice was firm.

"Perhaps you should talk to Ms. McQueen," Dane suggested.

"I will—when she returns. Now, if there's nothing else . . ."

Dane ended the conversation politely, but his temper seethed. He knew his request was out of the ordinary, and if the situation were reversed, he might act in the same manner as Lloyd Grady. Somehow he expected a little more courtesy from the plaintiff's counsel. Closing his eyes, he rubbed the strain out of his neck muscles. Why did he have the uncomfortable feeling that everyone in this Oregon town was trying

to hide something from him? Even his associate,
Fletcher Ross, couldn't be trusted. As for Lloyd
Grady, the respect Dane originally felt for the man
was beginning to dwindle. It was as if he were afraid
of something. Dane had noticed the dark glances he
had shot to his client during the deposition. And
Kirsten McQueen—there was a wariness in the depths
of her eyes that worried Dane.

The most expedient decision would be for Dane to
return to New York and forget Kirsten McQueen until
he could depose her again. Perhaps Harmon Smith, or
that assistant of his, Frank Boswick, could clear up
some of the enigma. But they couldn't help relieve
him of the attraction for Kirsten.

Her image teased his mind. Even now, when he
tried to concentrate on the peak of Mt. Hood rising
above the wispy clouds, he envisioned the slant of
Kirsten's mouth when she smiled, the gentle slope of
her shoulders and the provocative green tint of her
eyes. "You're a fool," he muttered to himself. His
broad shoulders sagged as he realized his motives for
staying on the West Coast. The lawsuit was an easy
excuse. He wanted to be with Kirsten McQueen
alone—as a man to a woman. Something in her
mysterious verdant gaze dared him to touch her.

"This can't happen," he warned himself, throwing
his clothes into his garment bag. *I have to remain
objective.* Dane's vexation was apparent in the furrow
of his dark brows and the pain in his eyes. It had been
a long time—maybe too many years—since he had
wanted, really wanted a woman. In the last six years
no woman had come close to reaching him the way
Julie had, and if the secret truth were known, he
preferred it that way. He didn't want another woman.
Ever. It hadn't been a problem. Until now. Instinc-

tively he knew that Kirsten McQueen could be the one woman who could change his life.

"It's too late for you," he scolded himself as he scooped up the keys to the rental car and zipped his garment bag. Rather than let the faded images of Julie enter his mind, he hoisted the bag over his shoulder, snapped the loose papers into his briefcase and strode out of the small hotel room.

He still had a few hours before his plane was scheduled to depart, but the thought of staying any longer than necessary in the room made him restless. He decided to have breakfast at the airport and hope to find a copy of *The New York Times* at a newsstand.

Once inside the rental car, he carefully maneuvered through the narrow streets of Portland's west side before crossing the Marquam Bridge and following the Banfield Freeway toward the airport.

It was time to return to New York and end all this folly about Kirsten McQueen. She was an enchanting woman, but he couldn't allow himself the luxury of seeing her. Not now. For the time being Kirsten remained the opposition, nothing more. And when the lawsuit would finally be resolved, Kirsten would hate him for defeating her. That was the way it had to be; there were no choices. He gripped the black steering wheel until his knuckles whitened. Damn Harmon Smith for dragging him into this mess!

Portland International Airport was a madhouse. The pilots for Westways Airlines had made good their threat to strike, leaving the fleet of jets grounded in eight western states. The sprawling terminal building, set on the banks of the muddy Columbia River was crawling with desperate travelers hoping to find alternate routes to reach their planned destinations. To complicate matters, there was the ominous possibility that the pilots for Flight USA Airlines would soon join suit. Their contract had expired yesterday and negotiations were rumored to be breaking down.

Kirsten edged her way toward the Westways desk. She had to pick her way between angry travelers, abandoned luggage and tired children. A red-faced woman turned on her heel, shouted an oath at the weary blond girl behind the counter and jostled Kirsten, who was approaching the tired reservation clerk.

"Is there anyone I could speak with concerning the strike?" Kirsten asked the blonde.

The girl turned her weary eyes in Kirsten's direction. She frowned slightly before replying. "You're Kirsten McQueen, aren't you?" A smile pulled at the corners of her mouth. "You won that big case against the television station, didn't you?"

"Not yet, I'm afraid," Kirsten responded.

"Hey—give me a break," an angry male voice interjected. "I need to get to San Francisco!" The balding man behind Kirsten shoved his way forward.

"What can I do for you, Ms. McQueen?" the reservation clerk asked, ignoring the protests of the angry man.

"I'd like to speak with Larry Whitehall. I'm doing a story on the strike."

"He's not here," the blonde said with a shake of her neatly cut hair. "He's supposed to be in Seattle, trying to renegotiate with the union."

Kirsten had guessed as much, but refused to be deflated. She needed a story, and this was by far the most newsworthy on the West Coast. "Then who's taking responsibility in Portland?"

Before the desk clerk could answer, the man behind Kirsten exploded. "Look, lady," he shouted, pointing an accusatory finger in Kirsten's face, "I don't give a damn about a story on the strike. I have to be in San Francisco by three o'clock, and I imagine the rest of the people in this line have better things to do than wait while you conduct an interview, for God's sake!"

"That's right," a female voice concurred.

The desk clerk shot a killing glance at the loud customer before returning her perturbed gaze to Kirsten. "I doubt if he has time to talk, but you might try to speak to Bob Ryan. He's probably at the United desk. United's agreed to try to move our customers."

"Thanks a lot," Kirsten said as she turned and nearly collided with the angry traveler.

"About time," the man muttered as he hoisted his elbows onto the counter. "Now, how the hell am I going to get to San Francisco in time for my nephew's wedding rehearsal?" he asked the blonde.

Kirsten didn't linger to hear the reply. Instead, she hurried toward the crowd centering itself around the red and blue sign indicating the desk of United Airlines, Portland's largest carrier. Kirsten's eyes scanned the sea of faces near the desk, looking for the ruddy complexion of Bob Ryan. Her gaze collided with the arrogant hazel eyes of Dane Ferguson. She felt her throat constrict. He was walking away from the desk and striding toward her. His eyes never left her face. The gleam of determination in the darkness of his glare promised an impending attack. His jaw had hardened and there was tension in his walk.

"Ms. McQueen," he said in a tightly controlled voice once he was near her. "I thought you were out of town."

"Pardon me?" She met his gaze unwaveringly, but the smile she attempted was thin.

"I called your attorney earlier this morning and he said that you weren't in Portland." He stopped only inches from her, seemingly oblivious to the confusion in the terminal.

A smile hovered on Kirsten's lips as she regained her composure. Seeing Dane here had been a shock, but she managed to recover. "I had planned to be away, but something came up."

"And you didn't bother to inform your attorney?" Dane was skeptical. A storm of doubt was brewing in his eyes.

"Lloyd's my lawyer, not my keeper." She drew her eyes away from the power of his gaze and looked past him, toward the United counter, where she spied Bob Ryan. "If you'll excuse me . . ."

A strong arm reached out and powerful fingers clamped over her forearm. "I'd like to talk to you."

She let her eyes drop to the fingers surrounding her arm before she met his gaze boldly. "Then I suggest you set up an appointment with Lloyd Grady."

"I tried that." His voice was cold; his jaw tilted arrogantly.

She was clearly skeptical. "And Lloyd wouldn't comply?"

"He said that he didn't want to bother you, that you were unavailable."

She inclined her head and her honey-brown hair fell away from her face. "Because that's what he thought," she explained. "I told you that I would talk to you again, and I will. I'm a woman of my word."

"Are you? Then why don't we talk now, in the coffee shop." His fingers relaxed slowly.

"I can't. I still work for a living, you know. But I'll be more than willing to talk to you when Lloyd agrees." She felt herself warming to him, and she couldn't allow that. As she took a step backward he reluctantly released her arm. Her eyes took in everything about him—his thick, slightly windblown hair, the crisp business suit, the power of his shoulders and his incredible, omniscient eyes. They were deepset and slightly brooding and Kirsten realized that there was little Dane Ferguson didn't see. A feeling of cold misgiving took hold of her, and she couldn't shake it.

"I suggested that we meet tomorrow or later this weekend," he suggested.

"And Lloyd said no?"

"Right."

"Well, look, Mr. Ferguson, I have a very important story to cover right now, and I think you would agree that I really can't discuss anything about the case unless my attorney is present." Out of the corner of her eye Kirsten noticed that Bob Ryan was walking briskly toward the glass doors of the modern terminal. A noisy throng of travelers and reporters followed in his wake. He looked as if he hadn't slept in days. Kirsten watched him leave the building. Within a few minutes he would be out of her sight and the story she was writing would have to be postponed.

"I'm sorry, Mr. Ferguson," Kirsten called over her shoulder as she hurried toward the doors of the terminal, but her words sounded false. She was relieved to be away from the power of the New Yorker's scrutiny, glad to put some distance between her body and his. As she half-ran after Bob Ryan, Kirsten told herself that it was just the thought of the lawsuit that bothered her. The hammering in her heart was the result of a number of things—the upcoming trial, the chaos in the airport terminal and her desperation for a good story. It had nothing to do with the fact that Dane Ferguson was a very intriguing man.

Three weeks later Kirsten was once again in the law offices of Grady and Sullivan. True to his word, Dane Ferguson asked for another deposition. He obviously hadn't been satisfied with Kirsten's answers to his earlier questions. Though she knew what to expect, Kirsten was still uneasy. This whole affair had dragged on too long and the thought of Ferguson's relentless questions worried her. She had only to remember the promise in his eyes when she had seen him in the airport. Too many nights she had considered those enigmatic eyes staring at her from across a courtroom. He would be deadly on a jury. The thought made her stomach twist with dread.

"What more could he possibly want to know?" she asked her attorney. Lloyd's wan smile was meant to be comforting.

"You tell me. You know as much as I do. Didn't he say anything in the airport?"

"I wouldn't let him."

"That's good. Besides, we'll find out when he gets here," the young attorney promised. Lloyd wished he could find a way to put Kirsten at ease, but he found it impossible to erase the deep lines of concern lining her flawless forehead.

"Can't we just say no thanks?"

"I don't think so." Lloyd's grin was nervous but genuine. He cared for Kirsten McQueen, and his dark eyes hardened at the thought of what Ferguson might try to do to her. "Look, Kirsten, we can't back down. Not now. We can't show the least little hint of weakness. You have to appear righteously indignant because you know that the truth is on your side."

"I don't want to perform, Lloyd. I just want to get it over with."

"I know," he consoled her with a worried frown.

When the secretary announced Dane Ferguson's arrival, Kirsten felt a stab of cold doubt enter her heart. There was something about the tall man from New York that took hold of her and wouldn't let go. Fletcher Ross had been easy to deal with because Kirsten disdained him. With Dane it was different. She respected the man and the honesty in his hazel eyes. It was difficult not to trust his lazy, easygoing smile or the gentle way he stroked his chin in confident reflection as he watched her. The trust he inspired was precarious. She had felt it the first time they met and again, fleetingly, at the airport.

He was waiting for her. He stood on the far side of the narrow room, leaning casually against the windowsill. His broad shoulders nearly filled the window frame. When she entered the room he straightened and adjusted his shirt cuff. There was warmth and humor in his knowing gaze as he appraised her, and Kirsten had the unlikely sensation that he was glad to see her. The trace of a smile curved his lips in the awkward moment when introductions were reaffirmed.

When seated across the heavy table from him, Kirsten attempted to relax. Though a professional smile crossed her lips, her spine remained rigid, poised for the verbal attack that was sure to come. Kirsten regarded Dane Ferguson as the enemy. Cool green eyes held his gaze firmly as if she were daring him to proceed with the inquisition.

"Good afternoon," Dane said. Fletcher Ross

cocked his head in Kirsten's direction, puffed on his cigar and watched the proceedings through narrowed eyes.

Kirsten returned the New Yorker's greeting and noticed that the court reporter was already in position to record everything that was said in the uncomfortable room. The smile on Kirsten's lips didn't falter. She reminded herself that she had to remain in complete control of the situation. Nothing Dane Ferguson or Fletcher Ross could say would rattle her.

"I'm going to pick up where we left off the other afternoon," Dane announced. He opened his briefcase and slapped some neatly typed pages onto the modern oak table. Kirsten remained silent, patiently waiting for the first of his questions. "I want you to tell me about your workday at KPSC," Dane suggested, resting his elbows on the table and propping his chin in his hands.

"What do you want to know?" Her poise never wavered.

"How did you get along with the station manager . . . what was his name?" Dane quickly perused his notes, but Kirsten suspected he hadn't forgotten the name. This was all part of the show—to lure her into saying something she would regret.

"Aaron Becker," Kirsten supplied with a tight smile.

"Right. How did you and Becker get along?"

"Very well, I think," she replied cautiously. "At least, professionally speaking."

A dark glance from Lloyd warned Kirsten that she was straying into forbidden territory.

"And personally?" Dane demanded, his voice controlled but a darkness gathering in his piercing gaze.

"We didn't socialize."

"Why not?"

The question wasn't necessary. "I don't see that the fact that I didn't socialize with Aaron Becker has anything to do with the case," she answered calmly.

Dane noticed the slight puckering of her delicately arched brows. He was getting somewhere. Quietly tapping the end of his pencil on the paper, he grinned slowly and in a manner meant to ingratiate himself to her. "I was just trying to establish the relationship that existed between you and your boss."

"It was professional—nothing more." She withheld the urge to tell him it was none of his damned business and managed to mask the resentment in her eyes.

He seemed puzzled. Thoughtfully he glanced at Lloyd Grady before returning his gaze to Kirsten's face. "But the other day, the last time we talked, you said,"—his dark eyes left her strained face to scour his notes—" . . . here it is: I asked you about dissatisfaction with your job and a memo to that effect and you responded with 'Some mention? You mean a memo from the station manager, Aaron Becker? Was that dated before or after I was let go?'" Dane paused before raising his eyes to hers. He contemplated the anger he saw in her eyes. "That question indicates that you and Mr. Becker had a misunderstanding."

"Not a misunderstanding really," she explained. "I wanted more involved assignments—"

"Such as?"

"Oh, I don't know." Kirsten tried to think. She wanted more examples than that of Ginevra, the most explosive issue, which had ignited her dismissal. "There were several big stories around at the time, and Aaron refused to let me cover them."

"Because of your age?" Obviously Dane doubted it. "Or was it because you were a woman?" He paused for dramatic effect. "Or was it something else entirely?"

"Kirsten has no way of knowing what went through Aaron Becker's mind," Lloyd cut in.

"Don't you?" Dane impaled Kirsten with his demanding gaze. Gold flecks sparked angrily in his eyes before his voice softened. "I just want to hear your side of the story, that's all." In the flash of an instant his entire demeanor had changed from that of inquisitor to one of an old, interested friend. Kirsten witnessed the ease with which he changed his expression, and her stomach knotted. He was good, damned good, and it was frightening. Very easily this man with the taunting hazel eyes and congenial smile could lure her into saying something she really didn't mean.

"Just before I was let go," Kirsten began evenly, her gaze never wavering, "there were several big stories. One was a political scandal involving a state senator, another was about a suspected drug ring south of Oregon City, and another involved a proposed site for a nuclear reactor near the coast. Aaron didn't want me to cover any of those stories."

Dane rubbed his chin pensively. Fletcher Ross pulled at the tight knot in his tie. Nothing seemed to be adding up to Dane. He felt the strain in the air. "Becker didn't want you involved because you were too old?" She didn't respond. "Forgive me, Ms. McQueen, but I'm having a little trouble understanding all of this." There it was again—the well-practiced country-boy charm, a direct contradiction to his expensively tailored suit and determined jaw. Kirsten wasn't fooled.

"Then perhaps you should ask Aaron Becker about it," she suggested.

"I intend to," Dane promised, leaning back in the oak chair and regarding her silently.

Fletcher Ross squirmed. The conversation was uncomfortable and the warm boardroom made him sweat. He could feel the dampness running down his back. Looking at his watch, he frowned before leaning over to Dane. "I think we've gotten all we need today," the portly man said, running nervous fingers through his hair. "I've got an appointment back at the office in half an hour."

"I have a few more questions," Dane responded, his determined tone warning Ross not to interfere. The authority in his intense gaze brooked no argument. Quickly his eyes returned to search Kirsten's intriguing face. "Why don't you think Aaron Becker let you work on any of those stories?"

"I don't know," she said. Her clear green eyes were shadowed. Dane knew he was getting near the truth.

"Was there another reporter better suited for the job? Say, one with more experience?"

"Not in my opinion."

"Isn't that a little lofty?"

"You asked; I told you the truth."

Dane looked to Ross for an explanation, but the Portland attorney averted his gaze. Fletcher Ross scowled and lifted his hefty shoulders, indicating that he thought Dane's line of questioning was of no importance.

"Were younger reporters given the choicest stories?" Dane asked, trying to understand exactly how the elegant woman seated sedately across the table from him felt.

"In one instance, yes. Another was given to a man who had been at the station about the same length of time as I had and the third . . . well, Aaron Becker didn't seem to place too much importance on Ginevra."

"Ginevra?" The name was vaguely familiar to Dane. Once again he turned to his associate, but Fletcher Ross shook his head, as if he couldn't fathom Kirsten McQueen or her interest in the town with the strangely familiar name.

Kirsten understood the exchange of confused glances, and the indifference on Ross's round face made her blood begin to boil. All of the anger she had fought so desperately to suppress threatened to erupt. Ross's attitude was the same as Aaron Becker's had been when Kirsten had first gone to her boss with ideas on the Ginevra story. For a reason she couldn't name, it was suddenly very important that Dane Ferguson understand. "Ginevra is the proposed site for another nuclear power plant. It would be Oregon's second, but no one at KPSC seemed to have much interest in it."

"Except for you," Dane guessed, returning his interested eyes back to Kirsten's incredibly beautiful face. She caught herself and didn't answer immediately. "Is the story significant?" Dane prodded, aware that Fletcher Ross was shifting in his chair and twirling an unlit cigar in his fingers.

"In this part of the country—yes. At least I think so."

"Why is that?"

Kirsten was about to expound on the subject, but understood the look of caution on Lloyd's even features. The perfectly groomed blond attorney spoke for his client. "This has nothing to do with the matter at hand. Ginevra is still in the planning stages and the only significance it bears on this case is that it was a small bone of contention between Kirsten and Aaron Becker."

Dane pushed up his sleeves, propped his elbows on the table and pressed his lips against his folded hands. His eyes reached out for hers in the thickening silence. "Ms. McQueen," he said softly. "Just why do you think you weren't allowed to cover the Ginevra story?"

"I wish I knew," she answered honestly, feeling the need to let this man understand her frustration.

"Then you think it might be more than just age discrimination?" His hazel eyes dared her to tell the truth. She felt herself wanting to reveal her deepest secrets before she shifted her gaze and forced her fingers to coil in resolution.

"I don't know what to think, Mr. Ferguson," she replied. "And—and I don't see that rehashing a dead issue such as Ginevra will help either of us with this case."

He raised a quizzical eyebrow. "You might be right, Ms. McQueen." Snapping his briefs into his case, he graced her with a smile. "I think that should do it," he stated, "unless, of course, I discover something else I need to discuss with you."

"Of course," she replied, settling back in her chair and breathing deeply for the first time all afternoon.

His dark, gold-flecked eyes swept the room to include everyone. "Thank you," he stated, rising to leave. A satisfied smile cracked across his rugged features and Kirsten had the impression that she hadn't seen the last of him.

Dear God, she thought to herself, *Dane Ferguson thinks of me as a challenge.* Involuntarily she squared her shoulders and her cool, emerald-colored eyes appraised him. *Well, if it's a fight he wants,* she promised herself as she watched his retreating figure, *it's a fight he'll get!*

Chapter Four

It certainly doesn't get any easier, Kirsten groaned to herself as she massaged her aching calf muscles. She was winded from the run and collapsed on the bottom step of the staircase, ignoring the gritty layer of sand on the rough boards. After completing four miles along the surf's edge, she realized that the early morning exercise had taken its toll on her. Her leg muscles ached rebelliously as she pulled herself upright and began to mount the weathered stairs that led from the beach to the cabin. Her lungs burned from her accelerated rate of breathing of the cold sea air. Between her own sweat and the thick fog, her hair had been reduced to a wet mass of dark ringlets framing a flushed face.

"Wonderful," she grumbled as she pushed the damp hair out of her eyes. "So much for keeping fit." The usual exhilaration she had come to expect from the run was missing, and she hadn't been able to dispel the ugly mood that had been her constant companion since yesterday afternoon. She paused to catch her breath and leaned over the bleached railing in order that she could survey the wet beach as if it were an uncompromising opponent. "Tomorrow I'll run five!" she promised herself, and slapped the railing with newly felt conviction. Her green eyes rose to pierce the fog, searching for the horizon. Try as she would, she was unable to discern the difference between the cold sea and the sky. The threatening gray waters of the Pacific seemed to bleed into the equally opaque sky. "Gonna be a storm, unless I miss my guess," she murmured, absently repeating the words she had heard from her grandfather time after time.

The wind coming from the north was raw as it blew against the strained contours of Kirsten's face. She hurried up the few remaining steps and walked briskly down the overgrown path leading to the house. With one hand placed against the weathered siding to support her, she pulled off her Nikes and placed them on a corner of the porch, convinced that she would need them for the next day's run. Why did she have such a lack of energy and enthusiasm for jogging? Kirsten had always enjoyed an early morning run on the wet sand. The smell of the salty sea had been invigorating.

Blame it on a lousy night's sleep, she decided, or better yet, on Dane Ferguson for robbing her of her slumber. She leaned against the doorjamb before entering the cottage. Why was it that she couldn't get him out of her mind? What was it about him that set him apart from the rest of the men she had met recently? She had considered the fact that she felt an eerie fascination for him because it was his task to defeat her—to prove her nothing more than a money-grubbing employee with an incredible chip on her shoulder. But there was something more to the intrigue she felt for him, something she couldn't define.

Though she had tried, she hadn't been able to put yesterday's inquisition or Dane Ferguson out of her mind. Shaking her head disgustedly while running her fingers through her tangled curls she entered the cabin and let the screen door bang closed behind her.

What was she attempting to prove by going after KPSC? Her righteous indignation and need for revenge had faded as she faced another time-consuming and costly trial. The thought of Dane Ferguson with his knowing eyes and sophisticated self-assurance only made it worse. No doubt the man would torture her on the witness stand, twist her words until the meaning was lost in a jumble of legal maneuvers and double-talk. Was it worth it? What had happened to her fire and determination? Weren't there any simple answers anymore?

She stepped into the shower and tried not to think about Dane Ferguson and the threat he posed. The rusty pipes groaned as she turned on the spray and felt the sharp sting of cold water against her overheated skin. Her cramped muscles began to relax.

Just when the water had warmed to a comfortable temperature, and she had finished washing her hair, she heard the phone ring. "I'm not interested," she said aloud, but the phone continued to shrill insistently. Her dark mood hadn't improved.

"Wouldn't you know," Kirsten muttered as she turned off the water and stepped hastily into her robe. She managed to make it to the telephone before the ringing had subsided.

"Kirsten, is that you?" Lloyd's worried voice called to her through the wires.

She closed her eyes. That was the trouble with Lloyd; he was so damned overprotective. As a lawyer it was a quality in his favor. As a man it was a fault to his detriment. Where did he get off calling her and then asking if it was she? "Yes, Lloyd," she said wearily. "It's I." She tried to mask the disappointment in her voice. It wasn't Lloyd's fault that she hadn't slept well or that she was doing a pretty good impersonation of Oscar the Grouch.

"Good." He sounded relieved.

"What's up?" she asked, toying with the phone cord and hoping that she wasn't dripping on the parquet floors. She attempted to ignore the fact that she was shivering and concentrated on the telephone conversation.

"It's Ferguson," Lloyd explained. "He's been looking for you."

Kirsten's heart stopped for a second. "Wait a minute—it's barely nine o'clock and I saw him yesterday. What do you mean, he's been looking for me?"

"Just that. He called this morning about eight. He asked me where he could find you." There was a note of anxiety in Lloyd's voice.

"I thought he would be back in New York by now."

"So did I."

"You didn't tell him where I was, did you?" Kirsten asked. Her anger had given way to dread. The last thing she needed was another confrontation with Dane Ferguson. He could read her too easily. His intense stare seemed to penetrate the darkest corners of her mind.

"Of course not," Lloyd replied. "I also reminded

him of the fact that I was your attorney and that you wouldn't talk to him unless I was present."

Kirsten leaned her shoulder against the wall, as if she suddenly felt the need for support. "Did that discourage him?"

There was a heavy pause. "I don't know, Kirsten," Lloyd admitted. "Believe me, I can't imagine why he would come looking for you, but he might. The guy's damned unpredictable."

"But not stupid, Lloyd. He knows that I won't say anything without your advice, so he would be wasting his time even if he did find me. From the looks of him, I doubt that he makes a practice of doing that." She almost talked herself into believing it, until she remembered Dane's penetrating stare. Those dark hazel eyes had silently made promises to her from across the table yesterday afternoon. She hadn't understood the meaning of those promises until now.

"I wouldn't think so," Lloyd replied, but he didn't sound convinced. "And you're right. Ferguson's not stupid—a far cry from it. All you have to do is look at his record to realize that."

"What record? You started to tell me about it once before, but you never finished. Just what is it that Ferguson's done?"

"I can't believe you don't remember. Think back. Remember the Stone Motor Company decision about six years ago?"

"Vaguely—something about a defective transmission?"

"Brakes. There was some controversy over a new type of disc brake that Stone had manufactured and put on its elite line—the Zircon. There was a class-action suit against Stone."

"And Stone Motors won."

"Right," Lloyd agreed.

"I take it that Dane Ferguson defended Stone," Kirsten guessed.

"You got it."

"Great," she mumbled, wondering if she was making an incredible mistake taking on KPSC. Her thoughts flew back to coverage of the Stone Motor incident. It was a national story—given to another reporter—but there was something out of the ordinary about the decision, an ironic twist or something. She couldn't remember. At the time she had been wrapped up in her own problems, the worst of which was that her marriage was falling apart. "Why didn't you tell me all of this before I met with Ferguson?"

"I thought you didn't need to worry any more than necessary."

"Hmph." Once again Lloyd had protected her. "Lloyd?"

"Uh-huh?"

"Wasn't there something else about that Stone decision, something . . . ironic?" She felt a twinge of dread at the question.

"I don't know if I would classify it as irony. Bad luck would be a better explanation," Lloyd allowed.

"For what?"

"Ferguson owned one of Stone's Zircons. It was his car, but one day, supposedly without his knowledge, his wife used the Zircon to take their kid to a doctor. They lived in Upstate New York, somewhere near Buffalo, I think. Anyway, the road was icy—"

"And his wife and son were killed when the car slid off the road and rolled down an embankment," Kirsten finished, remembering the details of the horrible accident. How could she have forgotten it? Now that she had met Dane, it all seemed so personal. A wave of nausea threatened to overtake her.

Lloyd's voice was grim. "That's right. To my knowledge it was never proven that the brakes failed. Too many other factors were involved to prove that the car was defective. However, the accident renewed the speculation and controversy that the Zircon was unsafe. Because of decreased sales, Stone was forced to quit manufacturing the Zircon the next year. The company nearly went bankrupt."

Kirsten was sickened by the story. She didn't want to feel any empathy for Dane Ferguson. She didn't want to feel anything for him at all. It was better that she remain detached and objective about him. That way she would remember that he was the adversary. She couldn't think of him as a man, a human being with problems of his own. The woman in her cried for him, conflicting with her instincts as a reporter which reminded her that he was dangerous. Any feelings for him personally were contradictory to her best interest.

Though she didn't want to know more about Dane, she was compelled to listen as Lloyd continued. "For a while no one heard from Dane Ferguson. He quit practicing law, and what happened to him in the next eighteen months is a mystery to me. Then he suddenly resurfaced in Manhattan with enough money to start a practice in the heart of the city. Within the last couple of years he's reestablished himself as one of the top lawyers in the nation."

"And he's decided to defend KPSC," Kirsten stated with a trace of disbelief. "Incredible."

"Or unlucky."

"What about both?" she suggested humorlessly. She told herself she didn't need this aggravation. If she were smart, she'd get out now, drop the case and look for a job in L.A. But the thought of Aaron Becker and the rest of the smug bigwigs at KPSC gave her an angry new determination. Let them call in the big guns from back east. She had the truth on her side!

"Look, Kirsten, I just wanted to warn you about Ferguson. If he does manage to find you, don't say anything!"

Kirsten drew in a deep breath. "How could he find me? You're the only one who knows where I am."

"But I'm not the only person who knows that you inherited a beach cabin somewhere around Cape Lookout," he reminded her. "Since you gave up your apartment, it wouldn't be too hard to guess where you're living."

"Lloyd, do you really think—I mean really think that he would track me down at the coast?"

"I wish I knew," Lloyd conceded. "It would help me immensely if I knew what that guy was thinking." There was a pause. "Hey, look, Kirsten, I've gotta run. Talk to ya later."

"Right," she agreed as she hung up the phone. She walked back to the bathroom and changed into her jeans and a sweater, letting her damp curls dry naturally.

She had only given up her apartment a few weeks ago, when she had decided to move, if only temporarily, into the small cabin her grandparents had owned. She had hoped that getting away from Portland would give her a fresh perspective and that it would take her mind off the trial. It hadn't. If anything, it had made the situation worse. Now she was that much closer to Ginevra, the site planned for Oregon's second nuclear power plant and what she considered the genuine reason she had been let go by KPSC. Her outspoken voice against the Ginevra plant had infuriated Aaron Becker. And when she had asked to do a story on the proposed site, he had flat-out refused, insisting that her opinions were biased. She had sworn to be objective about the story, posing both sides to the controversy, but Aaron Becker had been adamant, demanding that she continue covering local social events such as the Rose Festival and the opening of the recently restored Grand Theatre on Broadway. Within two weeks she was fired with only a few weeks' severance pay to sustain her.

Fortunately, she had saved some money while working at the station and there was the small inheritance her grandparents had left her. She supplimented her income by writing free-lance articles for magazines. It wasn't a lot of money, but she could live well enough on it because the small cabin overlooking the sea was unmortgaged. Now that she no longer had the rent on the apartment, finances weren't a major worry, although no one would believe her.

Her argument with KPSC wasn't over money, and the two hundred thousand dollars she had been awarded originally wasn't her primary concern. She wanted to see justice prevail, and she had no other means to fight KPSC than through a court of law. That she could be let go because she was a little older than the station would have preferred, and because she wanted to do more in-depth stories about controversial issues, certainly shouldn't be cause for dismissal. It would have been different if she had been a real pain in the neck, but she had always been a conscientious employee and had done anything her superiors had asked—until Ginevra. There was something about that proposed site that really bothered Aaron Becker. She could read it in his stony gaze the first time she had broached the subject: Ginevra was off-limits.

Why? To date, she hadn't had a satisfactory answer. She wondered if she ever would.

She threw on a light jacket and stepped into her shoes before going outside. Though the fog had lifted, a light drizzle continued to fall from the overcast sky. She ignored the signs of a storm and hurried down the slippery steps to the beach. In one hand she carried a short shovel and a bucket, the other was used against the wet railing for balance.

The tide was out and the sand near the water's edge was saturated with sea water. Though it was late in the day for digging for clams, Kirsten scoured the wet beach for the deep round holes that indicated a razor clam was buried beneath the surface. Spying the first hole, she dropped to one knee and began to dig in quick, short strokes. She was mindless of the tide, which would occasionally creep up on her, or the rain that had begun to fall. Her concentration was solely on the capture of the burrowing clam. When the sand became too wet and soft for the shovel, she tossed it aside and thrust her arm into the oozing hole until she felt the flat shell of the escaping mollusk with her fingertips. Her arm was wet and sandy to above her elbow, her sweater dirty and her jeans soaked by the icy salt water, but Kirsten didn't care. For the first time in weeks she wasn't brooding about the impending lawsuit.

Dane's eyes squinted in frustration as he stared at the crooked coast highway. He was traveling southward on the slippery asphalt two-lane road and the sudden rain shower impeded his speed. To the west, stretched out endlessly, was the gray Pacific Ocean. Frothy whitecaps rose on the choppy water, and the ominous color of sea and sky reaffirmed Dane's doubts.

He knew it was a mistake to track down Kirsten McQueen. There was no way he could justify his impetuous journey to the Oregon coast, but the short telephone conversation with Lloyd Grady earlier in the morning had nearly forced Dane to seek her. There was something overtly protective in Lloyd's voice, and without words the Oregon attorney had intoned that Kirsten McQueen was off-limits to another man. Dane had taken Lloyd's self-serving warning as a dare. He was certain he was making a grave error; he could feel it in his bones, but he was drawn to her, compelled to find her. Lloyd Grady's protective attitude toward Kirsten only served to reinforce Dane's determination.

He took a curve too sharply and the rental car slid into the oncoming lane. Regaining control of the car, Dane swore and forced himself to ease up on the throttle. He was behaving like a madman.

His hope that yesterday's deposition would end his desire for her had been frivolous conjecture. If it were possible, the confrontation yesterday had strengthened his need to be with her alone. He shifted the gears of the car as the road began to climb and he scowled at the threatening gray clouds in the distance.

Each time he had been with Kirsten, even fleetingly at the airport, he felt his attraction for her increasing.

"Damn that woman for getting under my skin," he muttered with a deepening frown. "This is lunacy."

Trying to ignore the fact that the risk he was taking might possibly cost him the case, Dane searched the dense foliage of twisted pines for the side street that would lead him to Kirsten's beach cabin. Never in his life had he been so foolhardy, but never had he been so damned possessed by a woman. Not even Julie. The passion he had shared with his deceased wife paled in comparison to the ache he felt for Kirsten McQueen. Maybe that's what happens when passion lies dormant for six years, he thought to himself. When it finally arises, the lusting ache becomes so heated that the memory of another woman fades.

He turned onto a private lane leading to a cabin on the cliff overlooking the sea. Or maybe the fact that Kirsten McQueen represented the opposition enticed Dane to her. That she was unavailable added to her allure. Whatever the reason, he was tempting fate by chasing her down, and the restless demons in his mind wouldn't let him forget it.

Kirsten had been at her task for nearly forty-five minutes when the tide started to come in. Her reward was six unbroken gold-colored clams. She spied a final hole in the sand. Kneeling near the small airway, she shoveled furiously before burying her arm past the elbow. Beneath her fingers she could feel the telltale movement of wet grains of sand. She pushed her hand deeper into the wet beach just as a frigid wave washed over her. Ignoring the discomfort, she closed her fingers around the sharp shell. So intent was she on her endeavor, she didn't notice the tall man standing only a few feet from the water's edge. His dark brow was furrowed, and his thick near black hair caught in the wind as he studied her with unconcealed interest.

"No one could accuse you of giving up easily," he observed loudly enough to be heard over the roar of the surf.

Kirsten's entire body stiffened. Though she hadn't seen him, she recognized the voice of the opposition. How many uncomfortable questions had it asked her yesterday—or a few weeks ago? The clam slipped through her fingers, cutting the soft flesh of her hand as it struggled for freedom.

"Damn!" Kirsten swore, retrieved her hand from the sodden pit and placed her fingers to her mouth to stem the flow of blood. She tasted salt and sand. Another wave threatened to catch her and she slowly rose to her feet, letting her eyes focus on the imposing figure of Dane Ferguson. So Lloyd had been right after all. The New York attorney had come looking for her. Though somewhat indignant at the thought, she was inwardly pleased. Why?

She half-expected him to be dressed in the most conservative business suit Brooks Brothers had to offer, and was surprised to note that he seemed at ease in a pair of faded jeans and a Windbreaker. He was still a formidable foe. No amount of dressing down could alter that fact, but at least he was more human—less lawyer.

"What the hell are you doing?" he asked.

She wiped her hands on her jeans and ignored his question. "Look, Mr. Ferguson," she stated, leveling her green gaze to his, "I don't know why you're here, but you may as well leave. I'm not answering any questions unless my attorney is present." Even to her the words sounded pompous and false, but she picked up her shovel and bucket, and with all the dignity she could pull together she started toward the stairs, telling herself that talking with Dane Ferguson could only spell trouble.

Dane was beside her in an instant. His long strides caught up to her easily. When she didn't look in his direction, he took command of the situation. Without warning, much like a cat striking, he took hold of her wrist and pulled her to a stop before examining the bloody tips of her fingers.

"Watch it," she growled. "What do you think you're doing?"

He paid no attention to the threat in her voice. "You're not very good at pretending to be tough," he accused her, looking intently at her hand. "What the devil happened here?"

She jerked her hand away from his, a pained expression hardening her soft features. "Why do you think they're called razors?"

"Wait a minute—what're you talking about?" he asked, holding his palms outward in a gesture begging her to be patient with him.

"These." She shoved the bucket under his nose. "They're called razor clams. Don't you have them in Manhattan?"

"Not alive."

The hint of a smile touched her lips despite her anger, and she rolled her soft green eyes expressively toward the darkened sky. "No," she mused aloud, as if she had just been told the answer to a complicated riddle. "I suppose you don't."

They reached the stairs. After setting her bucket on

the lowest step, Kirsten crossed her arms over her chest and leaned against the railing. The wind blew her hair away from her face, allowing Dane a glimpse of her ears and throat. "Mr. Ferguson," she asked cautiously, "what are you doing here?"

He looked tired but sincere. "I came to see you."

"That much I guessed," she replied, cocking her head and eyeing him suspiciously. He noticed the curve of her neck and the way her full lips pursed when she was puzzled. "I want to know why. I assume it's to ask me some more questions."

"Possibly . . ."

"The answer is no," she stated firmly. "Mr. Grady has advised me not to speak with you—under any circumstances."

"I'm sure he did," Dane allowed, placing his shoe on the lowest step of the staircase and leaning on his bent knee. His eyes narrowed as he looked toward the sea. It was as if he were seeing it for the first time. He noticed the white foam of the waves contrasting against the bluish-gray depths, the graceful flight of California gulls as they scoured the beach and the gnarled flat pine trees that clung to the edge of the cliff.

"Then why did you come here?" Kirsten inquired, her rage and indignation slowly giving way to curiosity.

Abruptly his dark gaze swept back to her. His smile was forced and conveyed a sense of self-derision. The wrinkles near his eyes had deepened. "I had a couple of reasons," he explained. "The first is that I don't completely buy the story you told me yesterday"—Kirsten started to interrupt, but he held his hand near his face in a gesture meant to cut off her angry

retort—"and the second is that I find you incredibly
. . . fascinating, for lack of a better word."

Kirsten wasn't easily persuaded. "Because I'm your
latest challenge—the opposition, so to speak," she
threw out, daring him to deny her assessment of the
situation. There was something about him that
touched her and made her aware of him as a man.
That alone irritated her. Kirsten didn't want to think
of the dark-eyed stranger with the mysterious smile as
a man. It was too disturbing. It would be wiser to
think of him only as the enemy.

He shook his head and his thick coffee-colored hair
ruffled in the wind. It gave him a boyish look that
lessened the severity of his angular features and
softened the intensity of his dark eyes. "The fact that
you're the opposition has nothing to do with it."

"And a cat really does have nine lives," she responded caustically. "Give me a break." She rubbed
her temple and tried to remain calm. "Look, Mr.
Ferguson—"

"Dane."

"Mr. Ferguson, don't try and con me. It won't
work."

"Oh, that's right," he agreed, mimicking her cynicism. "For a moment I forgot that you're a hotshot
ace reporter who knows all the angles."

Her dark eyebrows rose slightly, and a smile dared
to soften the pout on her lips. "Touché, Mr. Ferguson," she whispered.

"Call me Dane."

Once again he was rewarded with the elegant lift of
her brow. She didn't respond to his request, preferring to hear him out.

His ever-changing eyes held hers in a cold embrace.

"I just thought that it might be nice to meet you in less . . . confining surroundings."

"Forgive me if I'm skeptical," Kirsten announced with a slightly wicked gleam in her eye. "I tend to get this way when I'm around someone who's being paid to discredit me." She turned on her heel and began to mount the stairs.

Dane picked up the shovel she had left wedged in the sand before following her upward. He attempted not to notice how the tight wet fabric of her jeans hugged her buttocks, and grimaced to himself. How could a woman who was wet from head to foot, covered to the forearms in sand and still bleeding from an angry wound have the nerve to tell him where to get off? She appeared so damned lofty and self-righteous. Damn, but she was hard to figure out.

Kirsten managed to hold her tongue as she climbed the staircase. She wondered what she was going to do about the man a few steps below. He was obviously not easily discouraged, and she had to admit that she enjoyed his company—in a perverse sort of way. At least he wasn't dull!

At the top of the stairs she faced him, determined to make a final stand. When he stepped onto the path that led to the small cottage, she knew it was now or never. She was angry with him for seeking her and angry with herself for secretly being pleased that he would take the time and trouble to find her. His dark eyes were so mysteriously inviting, and if she were inclined to be romantic, she could imagine erotic promises in their vivid hazel depths.

His skin was dark, as if he had spent some time in the sun, and it was stretched tightly over the uncompromising contours of his face. He was a handsome man, she decided, but not in the classical sense. His features were too large and bold.

"I wish you would forget that I was the defending attorney," he stated.

"I'll bet."

He leaned on the handle of the shovel and his eyes drove deeply into hers. "Just think of me as any other man."

"A little hard to do."

He pulled an exaggerated frown. "I suppose it is a lot to ask, but it would certainly help."

"Help what—or whom?" He was beginning to work on her; she could sense it.

"Look, Kirsten," Dane began, and she bristled at the familiar use of her name. "I didn't come here to spar verbally."

"So you said." Her disbelief was evidenced in the dubious slant of her mouth.

"I really do find you extremely attractive."

There was a sincerity in his eyes that she wanted desperately to believe. She hated to admit it even to herself, but it was hard to ignore the fact that he was a very interesting man.

"And you expect me to believe that you came here just to get to know me better. This is a social call?" Her words were uncharacteristically caustic. What was the matter with her? Didn't she have the decency to be civil to this man?

A crooked smile exposed his straight white teeth. "Not entirely, no."

"I didn't think so." She managed to hide her disappointment under a veil of self-assurance.

"There are several things I have to discuss with you about the case."

"And you know that I can't. Not without Lloyd," she reaffirmed.

"This is strictly off the record." His voice was toneless.

"You've got to be kidding!" she exclaimed, but his eyes remained serious. "You can't expect me to believe that what you and I discuss will be kept confidential."

He folded his arms over his chest patiently. "As a reporter you sometimes heard things that were off the record." Kirsten nodded, her eyes still wide with disbelief. "And I expect that you never betrayed any of those confidences, did you?"

"Of course not! But this is a little different! We're talking about a lawsuit that I initiated against KPSC, and you're defending the station." She shook her head as if she hadn't heard him correctly. "You really can't expect me to trust your motives."

"I suppose you're right," he acquiesced, his features hardening. Once again his gaze traveled to the foreboding sea. The tidal waters were slowly encroaching on the sand. With each new wave the dark water came closer to the cliff.

A gust of wind blew across the ocean. Kirsten was chilled to the bone, and as the raw air rushed against her wet clothes her teeth began to chatter.

"You'd better go inside," Dane advised her, conscious of how uncomfortable she was. He cocked his head to one side and studied her with increasing interest. "You'll catch your death out here," he observed.

That's the least of my worries, she thought to herself. *You, Mr. Ferguson, are much more dangerous than anything I could possibly contract from the* weather. "That's an old wives' tale," she retorted. "People catch cold from viruses, not bad weather."

Dane's patience was pushed beyond his limit. He placed his hands squarely on his hips and glowered at her. "What is it with you, Kirsten? Are you mad at the world because you lost your job? Do you argue with every person you meet—or is it just me?" His mouth pulled into a grim line of disgust and his jaw hardened. He felt the unfamiliar urge to grab her shoulders and shake her.

"Everyone I meet isn't trying to mutilate my character," she threw back at him.

"You asked for that, lady. You initiated the suit against KPSC, not the other way around. You're getting only what you bargained for."

Her green eyes flashed. "And that doesn't include the harassment of the attorney for the defense knocking on my door! I'd hate to see how you would react if Lloyd Grady started questioning Aaron Becker without your knowledge."

"This is a little different."

"How?" she demanded.

A crooked smile touched his lips and his eyes gleamed with amusement. "Because I doubt that Lloyd Grady would find Aaron nearly as captivating as I find you."

She had to repress the urge to laugh at the image he brought to mind, but a twinkle of amusement sparked in her eyes. She was warming to the charms of the tall man from New York and her defenses were weakening.

Realizing that her behavior until this point had bordered on insolence, Kirsten felt a small stab of contrition. A drop of rain slid down her cheek, and she wiped it away with the back of her hand while she considered just what she was going to do about Mr. Dane Ferguson, attorney for the defense. He was persistent without being pushy, and there was something alluring about his ability to read her. It was as if he understood her innermost thoughts. His perception was precarious.

She wondered if it would hurt to talk to him as long as she steered the conversation away from the subject of the trial. Kirsten was a reporter, a good reporter, and she knew how to ask as well as avoid answering questions. Perhaps in talking with Dane she could extract information from him that might help her with her case against KPSC. It was possible that she could lure him into saying something he shouldn't. Just about anything could happen if only she dared take the chance.

Her most disarming smile formed on her lips and the suggestion of a dimple graced her cheek. "I didn't mean to be rude," she explained. "It's just that I'm a little wary of lawyers for the defense."

Dane made a sound of disgust. "And you should be," he said reluctantly.

"Then you understand why I'm cautious," she said, her green eyes warming.

"Certainly." Dane acted as if her worries were justified. He seemed to understand her position, and the woman deep within Kirsten wanted desperately to believe that he did. It was important that he realize how she felt.

"I'm sorry," she said, turning her back to him.

"So am I." His sincere words touched the deepest part of her, and she hesitated. Rotating to face him again, she had to struggle to hide the honest regret in her eyes.

"Under different circumstances . . ." she began, her voice fading into the wind.

He inclined his head and eyed her speculatively. He saw the hesitation lingering on her face, and he damned himself because he couldn't let go. He had the advantage and he pressed it. A cold blast of air from the sea caught in her hair and made her shiver. "You'd better go inside—warm up," he suggested, knowing just what to say to disarm her. He pushed his hands into the back pocket of his jeans and his eyes held hers in a gaze that promised her the moon.

He seemed so genuinely concerned. The raw force of the wind had colored his face. It was a kind face and a strong face. She felt as if she could trust her very life to this stranger with the enigmatic smile and slight accent. Her resistance ebbed with the soft look of worry in his eyes. She paused only slightly, and then smiled wistfully.

"If you promise not to turn the conversation to the lawsuit, I'll make you a cup of coffee."

"I don't want to trouble you."

You already have, she thought, *more than you can possibly guess.* "No trouble at all," she said, wondering about the risk she was about to take. "If you're lucky, I'll make lunch."

His eyes moved slowly away from her face to rest on the grimy bucket of clams. "I take it I'm looking at lunch."

She laughed at his exaggerated dismay and he thought her laughter was the most inspiring sound he had ever heard. "Don't they appeal to you?" she asked, her smile broadening as he stared at the clams.

"You appeal to me," he responded, sobering as he took her injured hand in his own. Rotating the slightly swollen fingers, he surveyed the wound. "As to the clams, I don't think I've ever eaten anything so . . . vicious."

An evil twinkle danced in her eyes. "Don't worry." She cocked her head in the direction of the bucket. "They'll get theirs. Just you wait and see what I intend to do to them."

"My pleasure," he mocked, echoing the haughty words of dismissal she had cast him at the first deposition in Grady's office. He pressed her fingers to his lips and tasted her wound. Kirsten's breath caught in her throat at the intimacy of the gesture. She had to sink her teeth into her lower lip when the tip of his tongue probed the sensitive skin. The warmth of his wet tongue on her chilled fingers might have been the single most erotic gesture she had ever experienced, and she couldn't help but wonder where it would lead. Her heart nearly skipped a beat before beginning to pound as wildly as the angry surf against the wet sand. Her eyes never left the darkened intensity of his. It was as if her gaze were controlled by the power of his knowing hazel eyes.

Slowly she withdrew her hand, attempting to ignore the shivering sensations he had inspired. Her voice was barely a whisper when she picked up the bucket and turned toward the cottage. "Please come inside," she invited him, wondering how much she was willing to offer this man, this adversary.

Dane smiled. Kirsten felt that it was the most honest smile she had ever seen. He took the bucket from her fingers. "Let me do this," he suggested, as if he had known her all of his life. The gesture was a simple deference to her womanhood, and yet she didn't feel threatened by it. Had any other man attempted to take the bucket from her, she would probably have been offended. Her ex-husband had proven to her how important it was for a woman to be able to stand on her own, without the need of a man for anything. But with this man—this stranger from New York—her feelings were vastly different, and if she stopped to analyze them, she would become even more uneasy than she already was.

Chapter Five

The size and condition of Kirsten's cabin were somewhat of a disappointment to Dane. When he had first discovered that Kirsten McQueen had retired to a private piece of property overlooking the Pacific Ocean, he had been expectant. For the first time since being introduced to the case, he had a glimmer of insight into the motives of the woman. Or so he had thought.

Dane had been certain that he would find her existing in an extravagant tri-level cedar house complete with hot tub, wet bar and sauna. He had been secretly pleased, hoping that the house would be an opulent symbol of her expensive tastes and lavish lifestyle. For his own peace of mind, Dane needed to know that there was a reason to believe that the intelligent woman he had met only a few weeks before would sacrifice any and all principles for the promise of a bundle of cash.

If he were honest with himself, he would have to admit that the case disturbed him—a lot. There was something about Harmon Smith's attitude that didn't ring true. It was almost as if the president of Stateside Broadcasting had a vendetta against Kirsten McQueen, and it didn't help that Fletcher Ross was a slimy excuse for an attorney. Dane hated the thought of trying to bail Ross out of the sticky mess his incompetency had created. So it would have been of considerable consolation for Dane if he could believe that Kirsten McQueen was the type of woman who would stoop to doing anything to continue living beyond her means.

Unfortunately, his theory had backfired right in his face. Yesterday afternoon he had surreptitiously noted that Kirsten was wearing understated but expensive clothes. The same had been true during the first deposition and at the airport. Her wardrobe indicated that she was accustomed to the finer things in life. But today she was dressed no better than any other beachcomber. Gone were the Dior suit and the Cartier bracelet. In their stead were well-worn jeans and a simple sweater.

Dane had expected to find an imported sports car in the drive. Once again he had been wrong. The small vehicle sitting near the garage was several years old, domestic and economical. The house proved no different. It was small, barely a cabin, and in need of several obvious repairs. It wasn't at all like the expansive estate he had hoped to find. The only thing of value was the land. With its sweeping view of the Pacific Ocean, the piece of property had to be worth a small fortune.

The entire McQueen case was becoming frustrating, damned frustrating, and the fact that he was becoming attracted to Kirsten didn't help matters. *You're going to slit your own throat,* he cautioned himself silently.

Kirsten eyed Dane with more than a hint of suspicion. She knew that he had been examining the grounds in an effort to understand her, and it made her uncomfortable. His practiced eye roved mercilessly over the weathered siding on the cabin, and she experienced the uncanny sensation that she was about to invite an unwanted intruder into her home.

"Are you going to stand out there all day?" she called from the porch after removing her shoes and opening the door. "Or would you rather come inside and dry off?"

Her questions brought his attention back to her. "What about these?" he asked, holding up the bucket of clams.

"You can bring them in; there aren't many."

"It makes a difference?" He seemed genuinely puzzled.

She was forced to laugh again. She hadn't laughed for a long time, and it felt wonderful. Dane appeared interested in the conversation, but she doubted that he gave two cents about clams or how they were cleaned. "If I've got quite a few, and the weather allows it, I clean them outside in a tray on the back porch. If not, I do them inside."

His suggestive smile was as enigmatic as it was contagious. "Then let me do the honors," he proposed before stepping off the front porch and walking briskly toward the back of the house. "You can work on the coffee—and make sure it's hot!" he called over his shoulder.

"Wait a minute . . . are you sure you know what you're doing?" Her voice trailed off as she realized that he couldn't possibly hear her over the whistle of the wind. The thought crossed her mind that she should help him with his task, but she decided against it, deriving a vengeful satisfaction at the thought of him tackling the unfamiliar work. "It'll be good for him," she thought aloud with a smile. "Character-building."

After cleaning and bandaging her fingers, Kirsten put a pot of coffee on the stove and started washing vegetables for a fresh spinach salad. From her vantage point near the sink, she had an unobstructed view of Dane through the window. She had to give him a little credit for the way he concentrated on his work. He looked up only once and that was to wink broadly in her direction. Why did the friendly gesture make her heart miss a beat?

He's an interesting man, Kirsten decided. He's full of surprises and contradictions. If it weren't for the fact that he was defending KPSC, she could envision herself getting involved with him.

By the time the coffee perked, Dane deposited the freshly cleaned mollusks on the kitchen counter. There was a twinkle in his eye and his grin was devilish. The clams were perfect; it was a professional piece of work. "Not too bad for a city slicker," he drawled with a western affectation and slow-spreading grin.

Kirsten glanced at the clams before impaling Dane with her curious green eyes. "Looks like you've had practice."

"A little. My uncle owned a fish market in—"

Kirsten held up her hand to cut short his explanation. "Don't tell me," she joked. "It looks as if I've been conned after all. And I swore to myself that I wouldn't be fooled by you. All that sophisticated loathing of live sea food—it was just an act."

Dane leaned against the counter and accepted a steaming cup of coffee. "But a good act," he protested. His eyes danced with merriment as he took a sip from his mug and observed her over the rim. He could get used to spending time with this woman, he determined, and wondered why in hell he had thought of that.

"Right. A good one," Kirsten agreed, shrugging her shoulders indifferently before turning her attention back to the scallions she had been slicing.

"You can't blame me for trying," he persisted. "I've got to find some way to keep you interested."

The rhythmic strokes of the knife faltered. "Is that what you're doing?"

"Isn't it?" he tossed back at her, his eyes narrowing just a fraction.

She reached for a dishtowel and, thoughtful, wiped her hands before turning to face him. Still holding the towel, she cocked her head and stared at him pensively, as if hoping for just a glimpse of his inner thoughts. "I wish I knew," Kirsten admitted with a sigh. "You've given me a lot of reasons for being here, but none of them entirely explain what it is you're looking for." She let out a long breath of air while she wondered if it would be wise to confront him with the truth—all of it. "Look, Dane, I know you're not going to want to hear this, but it seems to me that despite all the excuses you've come up with, the bottom line is this: You're here looking for something . . . some motivation for my lawsuit against KPSC, a reason to argue against the age discrimination."

Dane frowned into his cup and deep lines etched his

forehead. He hadn't counted on Kirsten's depth of perception. "All right," he acquiesced, "that much is true, at least partially." His dark brows blunted in concentration. "I'll be honest with you. I'm having a helluva lot of trouble believing the age-discrimination thing. It just doesn't wash with me. I think it's an excuse for a lawsuit, the only tangible reason you and Grady could come up with for taking KPSC to court."

"So you've determined that I'm just a woman with a grudge against her former employer and that I'm hell-bent to get some money out of KPSC and some national media attention for myself any way I can. You think I'm doing all this for money and publicity, don't you?" she charged, her eyes darkening and the skin drawing tight over her cheekbones.

"Aren't you?"

"Of course not!" she replied angrily. "Oh, what's the use . . ."

"What do you mean?" He had set his mug on the counter and was staring at her, listening to her every word, watching her slightest facial movement.

Kirsten's lips tightened over her teeth, but she refused to be drawn into the argument. It was too precarious and couldn't possibly help her. Perhaps she had divulged too much of herself to Dane already— and Lloyd had advised her not to say anything. "This isn't getting us anywhere," she whispered, attacking the hard-boiled eggs with a vengeance.

"That's where you're wrong."

"Aren't I always? Wrong, that is."

There was a sadness in his eyes, but he persisted, bringing his point home. "You really can't blame me, you know. You're only thirty-five, and on top of that you're beautiful . . . incredibly beautiful."

Her assault on the eggs slowed, and she paused

slightly, obviously affected by his words. She considered a response, but thought better of it, preferring to concentrate on the salad. It was safer, and she didn't have to look beyond his words to the meaning in his eyes.

"Kirsten, look at me." Dane was standing behind her, touching her lightly on the shoulders. The warmth of his fingertips seemed to flow into her as his hands gently coaxed her to face the questions in his eyes.

"Why can't you believe me?" she asked weakly. "What's so hard to understand? Carolyn Scott is only twenty-two."

"And from what I understand, she's just as qualified as you are."

"You can't believe that! Don't my years of experience count for anything?"

Dane studied the soft contours of her face and the determined gleam in her eye. "And so you think that you were discriminated against because of your age?" The worry in his gaze stated more clearly than words how deep his doubts were.

"You're forgetting that one jury already believed me," she countered, attempting to step backward and put some distance between her body and his. Strong fingers restrained her, held her fast.

"Are you sure they believed you, or do you think that just maybe they didn't believe Fletcher Ross?" he demanded.

"It's the same thing."

"You don't believe that any more than I do," he charged, a challenging light appearing in his eyes.

Her chin rose defiantly. "It doesn't matter. The point is: I won!"

He openly mocked her. "You, dear lady, may have

won the first skirmish, but that's only the beginning. The battle hasn't really begun."

She glared at him angrily, unable to hide the indignation in the misty green depths of her eyes. "What you're saying is that I haven't got a prayer because you're defending KPSC! Is that why you came here? To try to talk me into dropping the suit?"

A muscle in the back of his jaw tightened and his eyes darkened to a dangerous hue. "I just want you to be prepared."

"That's a lie, Dane. The last thing you want is for me to be prepared to face you. You're hoping to wrap up this case quickly and add another notch to your briefcase before flying back to New York!" She struggled to free herself from his grasp, but he refused to loosen his possessive grip on her arms.

"Just listen, Kirsten," he advised, giving her a shake.

"Why?" She jerked herself free of his imprisoning grip. "Just give me one good reason why I should listen to you!"

"Because I care about you."

"You don't even know me!"

"Oh, but I do . . . much better than you realize," he countered, leaning lazily against the wall and rubbing his chin.

There was a self-assurance about him that reinforced the meaning of his words. The proud manner in which he carried himself, the confident tilt of his head as he watched her and the bold, sharp features of his face served to remind her of who he was and what he represented: the opposition.

She took the offensive. "Reading my testimony . . . or analyzing my deposition doesn't give you any insight into me as a person."

"And you're attempting to ignore one very basic fact," he accused her. The slow movements of his thumb against his chin had halted and his eyes drilled into hers. Kirsten felt all of the muscles in her body tense as if they expected an assault. His gaze promised that once he began pursuing her, he would never stop.

"What fact is that?" she managed to say though her throat had become desert-dry.

His smile was self-demeaning. "The fact that I'm attracted to you."

"I don't see that attraction has anything—"

"You're trying to hide from the fact that I like you, Kirsten. And I'd like to know even more about you."

"To use in a court of law!" she whispered, trying to disregard the subtle traces of passion lingering in his eyes.

She closed her eyes for a second and tried to concentrate. The light and airy kitchen was becoming too intimate, the conversation too personal. She had to fight the power of his compelling gaze. All too easily she could believe anything he might say.

She felt the tips of his fingers caress the contour of her jaw. Her eyes opened and she was staring into the most sensual hazel eyes she had ever seen. The promises in their depths couldn't be denied; the questions they silently asked demanded answers.

"Why can't you believe that as a man I'm attracted to you?" he asked roughly.

She swallowed with difficulty, but held his gaze. The feel of his fingertips was seductive and dangerous. She reached upward and grabbed his wrists, hoping to slow the erotic assault on her senses. "Because I don't want to think of you as a man," she admitted.

"It's easier to consider me the adversary."

"Because that's what you are . . . can't you understand that?"

He drew in a ragged breath before pulling her close to him and wrapping his arms around her shoulders. He buried his face in the golden brown strands of her hair, drinking in deeply of the clean fresh scent. She smelled so damned feminine and she looked so innocently wise. "Sometimes things aren't as simple as we'd like them to be," he replied. "Sometimes feelings get in the way of the simple facts."

"That's just it, can't you see?" she cried, forcing her head backward so that her eyes could search his. "I don't want to have any feelings for you. I can't afford to trust you! The fact that you're here with me now is crazy—suicidal as far as the courtroom goes!"

The strong arms around her tightened. She could feel the hard muscles pressing against her, the warmth of his body enveloping her, the passion lurking in his gaze inviting her. "Don't confuse what happens between us with what will occur in court."

"That's impossible . . ."

Hazel eyes impaled her and held her fast. "Haven't you learned by now that nothing's impossible?" He searched her face, studying the feminine contours and wondering how futile his efforts were. There was no reasoning behind his interest in her, no logic. He had always considered himself a logical man, a man who pondered all the solutions to a puzzle before ascertaining the truth. But the puzzle of Kirsten McQueen was as much an enigma as it had ever been, and his attraction for her was entirely without thought or plan. He had known from the first time he had gazed into her mysterious eyes that warm afternoon in Lloyd Grady's office that the battle lines were drawn. This was a no-win situation.

Despite the arguments forming in his mind, he wanted her. More desperately than he had ever desired a woman did he crave Kirsten McQueen. Yes, she was beautiful, but it was more than her beauty that captivated him. It was the combination of beauty, wit, dignity and fire that held him fascinated. The feelings taking hold of him, driving him mad with frustration, were sparked by the allure in Kirsten's bright eyes and the trembling of her lower lip. The urges buried deep within him were primal and possessive. He wanted to claim this woman for his own.

Kirsten witnessed the play of emotions on Dane's face and realized that his thoughts had taken the same traitorous path as hers. She also knew that he was about to kiss her and that at this moment it was the one thing she desired most in the world. She wanted to be touched by this man. She needed to feel the power of his body crushed passionately to hers.

His head lowered and the warmth of his lips met the cool invitation of hers. She didn't resist, nor did she encourage him. His fingers twined in the honey-brown strands of her hair and he murmured her name. Her heart began to drum irregularly and she felt the rush of blood in her veins when his lips slid deliciously over hers. Warm urges, impassioned vibrations she hadn't felt in years, spiraled through her body and made her tremble at his touch. Involuntarily she leaned closer to him, enjoying the feel of his hard body aching for hers.

He sensed her reaction and he pulled her hair gently with his hands, forcing her head backward in order that he could press his wet lips against the exposed column of her neck. A shiver of anticipation scurried up her spine when his tongue found the delicate bones encircling the hollow of her throat.

"Don't," she pleaded, letting her eyes close with the delicious sensations he encouraged from her. It was a feeble objection, the final protest from a woman lost. . . .

His lips found hers again and this time the kiss they pressed against her was demanding. The gentle consideration for a woman Dane didn't know had disappeared as the fever within him had ignited. His hands pushed against the muscles of her back, forcing her breasts against the flat wall of his chest. His lips crushed to hers and her mouth parted to the insistent pressure of his tongue.

It had been so long since a man had caressed her as if he really cared. She gasped when the tip of Dane's tongue traced the serrated edges of her teeth and then probed farther, as if by physical exploration of her body he could understand her mind.

His hands stole up her back to finally rest at her shoulders. He pulled his head from hers and gazed deeply into her eyes, silently asking her questions she couldn't begin to understand. How much of herself could she give to this man?

"I want you," he said simply, and the honesty of his statement made Kirsten more aware of the danger therein.

"I know." She attempted to smile but was unable. The darkness in his eyes and the gentle pressure of his fingers promised sensuality and desire, surrender and satiation—if only she would take a chance.

"I want you more than I've ever wanted a woman," he whispered reluctantly, as if the admission itself were a betrayal. His warm breath moved her hair and his lips brushed seductively against her forehead.

"I don't know if that's enough for me."

His body became rigid. "What more could you possibly need?" he asked.

Kirsten's words were hesitant, as if she were unsure herself. How much of herself did she dare reveal to him and why did she feel the overwhelming yearning to make him understand her? Yesterday she wanted to hide from him; today she wanted to share her deepest secret with him. And yet she couldn't; she had to be cautious. Self-preservation had to come before physical desire. "I'm not asking for promises you can't possibly keep," she conceded. "And I don't expect to hear empty words of love."

His dark brows rose quizzically and his fingers rubbed the tired muscles near the base of her neck. "But there is something you want," he prodded. "Tell me—what is it?"

She tried to ignore the warmth of his hands on her skin, but she felt as if her entire body began and ended where his fingers touched her. "Dane, I have to know that you trust me . . . at least just a little. I have to think that this attraction isn't just because you consider me a challenge, an opponent that has to become a conquest."

"What are you trying to say, Kirsten?" he demanded.

"I need to think that what is happening between us isn't confused with what might happen in the courtroom."

The seductive movements of his fingers against her skin stopped. "I don't know what to think about you," he said.

"I don't understand."

"I think you're the one who has trouble with trust. If there's a problem between us, it's in your mind.

You're the one who can't let go and forget, not for one moment, that I represent KPSC." His voice was even, and though the words accused her, they didn't judge. It was a simple statement of the situation.

"How can I, Dane? Think about it. Think about who you are and what you represent." She tried to pull away from him, but he refused to let her go. "It's not as if you're an accountant or even *my* lawyer, for God's sake. You're the opposition!" The conviction of her feelings was evident in the confusion in her eyes.

"Would it be any easier if I were on your side?"

"I—I don't know." Dangerous sparks made his eyes appear greener than ever.

Her small fist opened and closed against his back. He could feel the tension and frustration coiling within her body. "You have nothing to lose, Dane. I have everything!"

His jaw tightened and he took a step backward, releasing her. She felt as if she might collapse on the floor, but she willed her body to remain rigid. His voice was cold and emotionless. "Do you want me to leave?" His eyes bored into her, waiting for her response. She knew that it was in her power to force him out of her life. She had but to tell him to go and he would never bother her again . . . until they met in court.

She shook her head regretfully, knowing she was making an unthinkable mistake. "Don't go," she whispered, inwardly longing for the protection and strength of his arms around her. "I—I don't want you to go." She paused and attempted to pull her scattered thoughts together as she raised her eyes to meet his unyielding stare. "The truth is that I think it would be best for you to leave, but if I'm honest with you, I'd have to admit that I want you to stay here."

"How long?" he demanded.

"What?"

His strong jaw hardened and the muscles in his neck stood out. "I asked you how long you want me to stay. A few minutes? For lunch? The rest of the afternoon? The night?"

She leaned on the cane back of one of the kitchen chairs. Her fingers dug into the hard wood. "I don't understand—why are you angry?"

"I don't like being toyed with," he stated flatly.

"That makes two of us," she tossed back.

The anger he had vainly tried to control snapped. The rugged features of his face became threatening, the hazel eyes bold. His lips thinned into a grim line of frustration. "I'm having one helluva time reading you. One minute you're vicious, the next seductive. I don't know whether I'm coming or going."

She lifted her head above his angry insinuations. "Don't give me that! I don't believe for one moment that you don't know exactly what you're going to do, and I'm appalled that you would expect me to. This entire charade"—she made a sweeping gesture with her arm, as if to include everything which had happened between them—"was just an act, and probably well-rehearsed." Her eyes had hardened to opaque emeralds. "I'll bet that you know exactly what your next move will be."

"With you? That would be impossible!"

"Aren't you the guy who just told me nothing's impossible?" Her lips curved into a vengeful smile and she hoisted her chin a little higher into the air. "And aren't you the man being paid an outrageous legal fee to prove that I'm nothing better than a money-mad disgruntled employee who would like nothing better than to see KPSC, and, for that matter,

Stateside Broadcasting Corporation, go down in a ghastly conflagration of national publicity and ridicule!"

Dane watched her angry display and found his rage giving way to awe. She understood the defense's position much more clearly than he would have guessed. "Since you understand me so well," he encouraged her, managing to hide his sarcasm and attempting to seem less interested than he actually was, "why don't you tell me why Stateside Broadcasting Corporation is involved?"

"Beats me," she admitted.

"But surely you can hazard a guess?" he went on.

"I don't know why. They're your clients—the men responsible for sending you here in the first place." She turned her attention back to the salad and then went to work breading the clams.

"So why do you think Harmon Smith is so interested in you?" Dane continued.

She slid a glance in his direction. The conversation was ticklish; she would have to be careful. But at least it had turned away from the personal confrontation between a man and a woman. "So you want my opinion strictly off the record?" she asked.

"Right."

"I wish I knew," she conceded, casting another sidelong glance in his direction. He was watching her, studying her with those intense hazel eyes. She had to be cautious in her answer, hoping to tell from his reaction if her suspicions were founded. "If I had to come up with a reason, I'd say that Stateside must be afraid of me. Why else would they send in their big gun from back east?" His eyebrows had quirked when she had referred to him, but other than that one show of emotion, Dane's face had remained unreadable.

"And why would a national broadcasting corporation be afraid of one woman?"

"Because of what I represent, I suppose." She placed the pan on the stove and hesitated for a moment. "They must think that they have to make an example of me."

"So they hired me?"

She shrugged her shoulders. "I guess."

Dane asked his next question very carefully, for he thought he might finally understand just a little of the puzzle. "What about Fletcher Ross?"

"What about him?" Just the thought of the heavy-set man with his thick jowls and habitual cigar made Kirsten's stomach sour. Her eyes were innocent when she raised them to meet Dane's inquisitive stare.

"I'm not one to upstage one of my associates . . ."

She smiled thinly. "Tell me another one."

"What I mean is, why would KPSC hire Ross in the first place? He doesn't come off very polished."

"You don't have to mince words with me. What you're trying to say is that he's a long shot from first rate. You know it and I know it."

"So why doesn't KPSC know it?"

Kirsten frowned as she prodded the clams and placed them on a platter. "They do, I suppose."

"But they would still hire the man?" Dane was clearly dubious but very interested.

"Sure. He's got a long-term contract. Besides, I think he's got money in the station . . . or something."

"An investor?"

Kirsten thought for a moment before placing the dishes on the small antique table. "I don't know really. Anyway, don't quote me. Remember, we're still off the record." As if realizing how risky the conversation had become, Kirsten managed to change the subject. If Dane noticed her reluctance to discuss the station, he hid it well. "We'd better sit down," she suggested. "If we don't eat this soon, we'll have to call it dinner."

Most of the meal was eaten in silence. Kirsten should have been ravenous but found it difficult to enjoy the efforts of her labor. Having Dane in her home made her uncomfortable. His watchful eyes noticed everything, and she couldn't help but feel that he would use anything he could find to his advantage. It had been an incredibly stupid mistake to allow him into her home and the fact that she was attracted to him only made it that much worse. He was smooth— too smooth.

"You haven't lived here long," he said, pushing his plate aside.

"A few weeks."

"Did you buy the place?"

She shook her head. "I inherited it from my grandfather. He lived here until he passed away last winter."

"Is this where you came to spend your summer vacations?"

Kirsten smiled wistfully, remembering the hours spent with her grandfather on the beach. "Some of them—when both Grandpa and Grandma were alive."

"What about the rest of your family?" Dane asked, leaning back in his chair. His eyes were warm and familiar. The lingering traces of suspicion had disappeared.

"I have one sister; she lives in Idaho near my parents," Kirsten replied with a thin smile.

"So what brought you to Oregon?"

He seemed to ask the question innocently, but Kirsten reminded herself that he already knew the answer. "I've always lived here."

"But not your parents?"

"They moved to Boise later . . . after I had graduated from college." Her voice faded as she remembered those stormy years when she was married to Kent. Talking about that period of her life always made her uneasy, and though Dane was obviously just making small talk, she felt nervous, as if she were once again on the witness stand.

She picked up the dishes and took them to the sink, hoping that the conversation had ended. She didn't need to be reminded how alone she had felt when her parents had moved to Boise. Her marriage was slowly beginning to fall apart, and she had no one in whom to confide. The one thing in which she had taken consolation had been her job, and even that had eventually gone sour.

"You must have been the favorite grandchild," Dane observed as he rose from the table and helped put the dirty dishes on the counter.

"I don't think my grandparents played favorites."

"But you inherited the cabin."

"Actually my sister and I both did. She didn't want it, so I bought her out." Once again she felt as if she were revealing too much to this man. It was so easy to be honest with him—no wonder he had earned his reputation for winning in court. It was hard to discern between the lawyer and the genuinely interested and charming man. "The dishes can wait," Kirsten announced, walking toward the living room.

"Why didn't she want it?" Dane asked, knowing that he was disturbing her but determined to find out as much about Kirsten McQueen as he could.

Kirsten bristled, and her temper got the better of her. "Is it really any of your damned business?" she returned. "Why is it that you lawyers can never give up? Ever since you got here it's been one question after another!" She jerked her jacket off the hook near the door and turned her icy eyes on him. "You're all alike!" With her final insult she pulled the door open and started outside.

"Are you comparing me to Fletcher Ross?" Dane asked with an amused smile. *Damn the man, he knew how much he outclassed the likes of Ross.*

"You can take it any way you like!" She hurried down the steps of the porch and headed toward the garage. He was beside her in an instant and hadn't bothered with a jacket. Wind and rain from a blackened sky poured down on him.

"What're you doing?"

"Getting firewood before it really gets dark. I want to be prepared just in case we . . . I lose power!"

"Let me help you."

"I don't need your help," she shouted at him. The noise of the wind and the crashing surf made it difficult to hear. She pushed the garage door open with her shoulder. It was dark inside and smelled of dust and dried fir. She threw several chunks of fir and oak into a basket standing near the door.

"Being an independent woman doesn't include having your pride stand in the way of common sense," Dane advised as he took the heavy basket from her arms and turned toward the house.

She followed behind him with an armful of dry driftwood. "And you can take your male philosophy on life back to New York with you."

Once inside the cabin, he placed the basket near the brick fireplace and dropped several pieces of fir onto the smoldering flames. As the fire caught it cast a warm light into the otherwise dark room. When the flames were to his satisfaction he rose and dusted the palms of his hands on his jeans. Raindrops slid from his wet hair down the severe angle of his cheek. His eyes had turned as stormy as the sea. "I didn't come here to judge you."

"No, you're saving that for later, when you can really do a job on me in the courtroom," she accused him. The light from the fire caught in her angry green eyes and gave her soft hair highlights as warm as the golden flames.

His lips tightened into a tired frown. "If you let yourself, you can become a very lonely woman."

"If I do, it's my choice," she asserted.

"I don't understand why you're so angry with me," he stated, "but unless I miss my guess, I'm just an easy target. You're angry with men in general, aren't you?"

She held back the hot retort threatening to erupt. "It's not so much anger, Dane, it's freedom. I don't need a man telling me what to do. Nor do I need a man poking his nose into my personal life."

"Why don't you be honest with yourself, Kirsten," Dane replied, taking a step nearer to her. Steadfastly, she held her ground, refusing to be intimidated. "You're afraid of me . . . afraid of what I represent . . ."

"I'm not afraid of anyone at KPSC," she reaffirmed, the fire in her eyes emphasizing her assertion.

"I'm not talking about KPSC! Why can't you forget about the damned suit for a few minutes?"

"Because I'm talking to the defending attorney!"

"And the minute you forget that fact you think you've lost!" he charged, his penetrating eyes dark.

"Something like that, yes."

"Oh, lady," he whispered, coming close to her. There was a pain shadowed in the depths of his eyes. "If only it were that simple." He folded her gently into his arms, and she didn't resist, somehow finding an unknown comfort in the feel of his body stretched against hers. His head descended and his lips sought hers. She trembled in anticipation and accepted the touch of his mouth on hers. The soft pressure of his tongue gently parted her lips and she gave herself willingly to the bittersweet yearnings of her body.

Their tongues met, retracted and met again to mate in an intimate dance known only to lovers. She savored the taste of him, drowned in the smell of fresh raindrops against his skin, relished the warmth of his body powerfully holding hers.

He kissed her eyes and let his wet lips touch each cheek. His hands pressed against the small of her back, rubbing her in anxious circles of desire.

"Let me touch you," he whispered, and the raw tone of his voice let her know of his frustrated longing. When she didn't respond, he brought his lips back to hers and his fingers found the hem of her sweater. Slowly they crept up her back, tracing the soft muscles and inspiring a warmth within her she tried valiantly to deny.

"I don't think . . ."

"That's right, Kirsten, don't think . . . for once don't think, just feel—let yourself go."

His fingers caressed the slope of her spine as they inched upward. His lips were warm and persistent, his hands gentle and coaxing. They inched up her rib cage until they felt the weight of her breast. She gasped when his hand pushed upward on the firm flesh and a soft sound escaped her as he lifted the sweater over her head.

Involuntarily she crossed her arms over her breasts, as if to protect herself. He took hold of her wrists and forced her hands back to her sides. His eyes were gentle but determined. "Don't hide from me . . . you can't." Once again he held her fiercely to him and kissed the inviting swell of her breast. Her heart raced furiously, pounding in her head, warming her blood. Her breathing had become shallow, as if each breath were stolen from her lungs. A thousand reasons to pull out of his insistent embrace entered her mind, but fled when just as many excuses to stay bound to him argued in his favor. She wanted him to touch her, though she knew it was a mistake. She needed to feel his hands caressing her.

He took each manacled wrist and brought it to his lips, trying to physically ensure her that he wanted only what was best for them. With gentle prodding he kissed her again, and when he let go of her hands she didn't resist but wound her arms around his neck. She shivered as if from the cold, but the heat rising within her was the cause.

She felt the muscles in his arms flex as they wrapped around her and the soft hair of his forearms brushed invitingly against her naked back. Slowly he shifted his weight until he forced her onto the floor. The cool parquet sent a chill down her spine, but the warmth of the man leaning over her, pressing hot lips against hers, made her cognizant of nothing but him and the power of his passion.

"This is crazy," she sighed, watching as the firelight flickered in his eyes.

"This is right . . . you don't have to think of anything else." His lips lowered and lightly kissed the hollow of her throat before toying with the clasp of her bra. She could feel her breasts strain against the flimsy fabric when his tongue would touch her skin. Her nipples had hardened to stiff dark peaks rising against the sheer white lace. She quivered when his tongue rimmed her nipple, wetting the flimsy fabric and leaving a cool impression on her skin. The fires within her burned more ravenously, and a thin film of sweat began to collect on the small of her back.

"Oh, Dane," she murmured, her voice breaking with frustrated longing. "How can this be happening?"

"It's happening because you want it to," he whispered, his words ringing with the truth she felt in her heart.

"But I can't . . . I just can't," she cried, her small fist pounding relentlessly on his back, as if by striking him she could deny the feelings bursting within her.

"You have to let go."

"Oh, God, if only I could," she whispered, clinging to him and holding back the tears of frustration begging to be shed.

As if he finally understood that he was pushing too hard, Dane gently released her, keeping his hands on her shoulders, forcing her to look into his eyes. The strain on his face showed how he was willing back the tides of passion rising within him. He fought to ignore the powerful ache of desire that refused to subside. His voice was hoarse, his skin stretched taut over his cheekbones. "Don't get me wrong, Kirsten, I want you more than I ever thought possible. But I would never rush you into anything you might not be able to handle."

"What I want and what we can have are two

different things," she replied, her green eyes pleading with him to understand her. "I can't deny that physically I desire you . . . but I want more than physical satisfaction."

He pushed back a wayward lock of his dark hair and stared at the ceiling, as if by studying the exposed beams he could come to terms with his traitorous feelings. "All right. That's for you to decide. I'm not about to get involved with a woman who can't accept a relationship for what it is."

"That's the problem, isn't it?" she asked. "You call it a relationship and I call it sex. In my book, a relationship is much more involved than one afternoon in front of the fire."

"Is that all it means to you?"

"No," she shook her head. Streaks of amber shone in her hair. "There's more to it than that," she admitted. "Under different circumstances . . . maybe things could have worked out. But I have a lot of trouble dealing with the fact that you are, for all practical purposes, hired to be here by KPSC."

"Not here, not with you, not now."

She closed her eyes. "If only I could believe that."

He eyed her speculatively. His voice was low. "I think I'd better go," he said softly. "Until you can understand that I'm a man as well as an adversary."

"Maybe when this is all over—"

"Be serious, Kirsten. When it's all over, one of us will be the winner, the other will have lost. Do you honestly think that either one of us will be able to overcome that?" he asked, handing her the discarded sweater. She took it and held it protectively over her breasts.

"Then I guess we're at an impasse?"

He didn't notice the desperation in her voice. Nor

did he see her vain attempt at poise. She felt as if he had come into her life and shattered it into a thousand pieces, but she managed a thin smile.

"Kirsten," he said. "I'd like to say the things you want to hear. Hell, I'd even be glad to make promises that I can't possibly keep. But I won't. I think too much of you to lie to you, and I expect the same in return." He touched her lightly on the chin, but she pulled her head away, afraid that his familiar touch would break the dam of tears burning behind her eyes.

"All I've ever wanted from you was the truth," she replied.

"Okay, so now you've got it. I hope you can live with it." He rose and reached for his jacket. "Goodbye, Kirsten."

He didn't wait for her response. In a quick movement he turned on his heel, opened the door and was gone, leaving the room more empty than it had ever been. Kirsten's throat swelled, but she refused to let go of her tears. She'd been through worse times than this, and she would weather this storm.

She ignored the sound of the car engine catching and told herself it was for the best when the noise had faded in the distance. The next time she would see Dane Ferguson she would be prepared. She wouldn't be so foolish as to let him see the soft side of her again. As far as that man was concerned, she had learned her lesson, and somehow she would be able to face him in the courtroom—that much she vowed.

Chapter Six

The stormy afternoon slipped slowly into evening. Kirsten managed to finish a few tasks around the house. She paid the bills, cleaned the kitchen and tried to concentrate on rewriting a story about the decline of timber sales in Oregon, but found that the facts and figures in the recent slump didn't interest her. Her traitorous thoughts continued to return to the magnetic power of Dane's hazel eyes and how easily she had been captured by his seductive spell.

With a futile sigh she put the plastic cover on her typewriter and stripped out of her clothes. After a quick hot shower Kirsten slipped into her warm velour robe and poured herself a glass of Chablis. She stretched out on the small, slightly faded Oriental rug that covered the hardwood floor near the fireplace. Her back was supported by the couch and she stared restlessly into the amber flames of the dying fire.

"You're a fool," Kirsten whispered to herself as she

sipped the cool wine and noticed the blood-red reflection of the coals in the crystal goblet. "You should have listened to Lloyd Grady and sent Dane Ferguson packing. What's the use of hiring an attorney if you're not going to listen to his advice? Anything you said to Ferguson will be used against you, sure as shootin'."

She sighed deeply, set down the glass of wine and let her eyes wander through the cabin. It was her home and she loved it, but tonight it seemed incredibly empty. It was as if Dane's presence of a few hours had altered the warmth of the interior. Everything looked the same, but the once cozy rooms felt lifeless.

"Honest to God, Kirsten," she muttered. "You're acting maudlin and morose, just because of one man." She chided herself repeatedly for being the kind of woman she abhorred before reaching angrily for the newspaper, grabbing her reading glasses from the coffee table and slipping them onto her nose. Expertly her eyes roved over the newsprint as she studied the local news, hoping to find an article of interest.

On the first page of the business section was an article on Ginevra and Kirsten's eyes moved hungrily over the text. She hoped to discover something new about the proposed nuclear site but was disappointed. The article was filled with the same old controversy, without any new facts or even a new editorial slant. However, the name of the journalist who had covered the story wasn't familiar to her, so she tore the page from the paper and set it aside. Maybe when the lawsuit was behind her, she would be able to write an in-depth story on Ginevra without the fear of repercussions in court.

When the lawsuit was behind her. Would there ever be a time when she wouldn't be caught in a legal battle with KPSC? She shook her head and reached for the glass of wine. Right now it seemed as if the lawsuit would never end. She wondered how the as yet unselected jury would vote when they heard her side of the story.

Would Dane Ferguson make her appear nothing more than an irrational woman harboring a secret vendetta against KPSC? Was he capable and cruel enough to make her look like an incompetent two-bit reporter looking for a quick, easy buck? She closed her eyes against the vivid image of Dane, dressed in a conservative suit, smiling charmingly to the jury and pointing a condemning finger at Kirsten.

"Oh, dear Lord," she whispered aloud, "why did I start this?" After mentally reviewing her conversation with Dane earlier in the day, she decided that she hadn't said anything that was damaging to her case. However, if Dane decided to twist her words around, anything she might have casually mentioned might hurt her. And she had foolishly thought she could extract information from him!

To dislodge the disturbing thoughts, Kirsten pulled herself to a standing position, stretched and listened to the sounds of the coming night. The storm had continued to rage throughout the afternoon and evening and the rush of the wind had at times been strong enough to rattle the panes of the windows facing west. Kirsten walked across the small room and sat on the smooth wide sill of the bay window to peer into the darkness. Floodlights secured to the cliff cast eerie light onto the angry Pacific Ocean. Spray from the sea as it crashed against the rocks protecting the beach splashed upward into the blackened sky before running in frothy rivulets back to the turbulent ocean.

A movement of unfamiliar light caught in Kirsten's

peripheral vision and she turned her head away from the view of the wild ocean. Pale headlights in two thin streams of illumination were advancing down the twisted lane toward the cabin. Kirsten squinted into the night and tried to determine the make of the approaching car.

Her elegant eyebrows lifted as she recognized the rental. Dane Ferguson was back!

Trying to ignore the sudden dryness that had settled in the back of her throat and the fact that her stomach had constricted into uncomfortable, tight knots, Kirsten waited until she saw Dane pull himself out of the car and hurry head-bent against the torrent of rain, toward the front porch.

Kirsten reached the door just as she heard his loud, impatient knock. Standing aside to allow him to enter the room, she opened the door and managed to hide the confusion gripping her.

"What happened?" she asked, staring at his wet clothes and the dirt streaked across his face. He met the questions in her gaze directly and she noticed something in his disturbing gaze that she hadn't seen before. It was pain. Deep and raw. The kind of agony that was seldom unhidden.

"An accident—three cars piled up near a bridge that had washed out." His voice was low and strained with emotion. When he wiped the rain off his forehead with his palm, Kirsten noticed that his fingers were unsteady. It was something she hadn't expected to find—a crack in the firm resolve of Dane Ferguson.

"Wait a minute," she stated, and hurried into the hallway to search the linen closet. Within a few seconds she was back and handed him a dry bath towel. "Why don't you go into the bathroom and

. . . clean up." She eyed his mud-covered jeans suspiciously. "Do you have a change of clothes with you?"

"In the car."

"Go out and get them and then you can shower. I'll make some coffee and—have you eaten?" Her eyes rose to his, but he didn't answer immediately. "Doesn't matter. I'll throw something together—"

"You don't have to go to all this trouble."

"Of course I do," she asserted. "You're here, aren't you?"

"I could go to a motel. . . ."

"The nearest one is miles away," she replied. "Just go get your clothes and clean up." Kirsten turned toward the kitchen as if she expected her commands to be obeyed. Her heart was beating unnaturally in her chest. The last thing she had expected was to have Dane return, but now that he was here, she found it inconceivably painful to think that he might once again disappear into the darkness.

She heard the door close as he went outside. Desperately she counted the seconds under her breath until he reentered the house. Just as she put the coffeepot on the stove, she heard the sound of running water from the bathroom. It was a warm and comforting thought to know that he was with her—one man and one woman caught together in the wild fury of the storm.

By the time she had poured the coffee and the chowder was simmering on the stove, the water in the bathroom was no longer running. She carried the hot food into the living room and set the tray on the coffee table before taking a chair near the fire and waiting.

Dane emerged from the short hallway leading to the bathroom a few moments later. His hair was still damp but neatly combed, and all of the traces of dirt were gone. He had put on clean corduroy pants and a sweater. When he looked at Kirsten he managed a tight smile, but she noticed that the haunted look in his eyes hadn't disappeared. There was something about that small glimmer of vulnerability that touched the deepest part of her.

He accepted a cup of coffee and took a long swallow of the hot liquid. "Thanks," he whispered, and his eyes never left hers as he drank from the steamy cup.

"I didn't mean to come racing back here," he said as if in apology.

"I know." Her words were sincere and encouraging. She sat across the room from him and the small coffee table separated them. She had crossed her legs and one slim calf parted the folds of the downy white robe.

He had to force his gaze from the enticing leg, back to the soft contours of her face. "I spent a little time driving up the coast before I started inland. I wasn't very far out of Cannon Beach when I came to the accident. . . ."

"Where the bridge had washed away?"

Dane nodded thoughtfully. He frowned into the coffee cup and a muscle in the back of his jaw tightened. "I don't think there was a car on the bridge at the time, but no one knows. Apparently, the driver of the first car saw that the bridge had buckled and slammed on her brakes. The pick-up following her reacted a little too slowly. When the truck slammed into the car, the car slid down the embankment into a ravine." He paused for a sip of coffee to quiet the rage of wretched indignation boiling within him.

"A woman and her child were trapped in the car,"

Dane said, suddenly pursing his lips. "We were able to get them out. . . ."

"But they were badly hurt," Kirsten guessed.

Dane shrugged. "The boy will be okay. At least the paramedics seemed to think so when they got to the bridge. But they weren't as optimistic about the mother." He finished the cup of coffee before continuing. "The state police asked that everyone at the scene give his name and phone number, in case there were any questions about the accident. When I told them I was from out of town, they asked me to give a local number where I could be reached—"

"And you gave them mine?"

"Yes." After setting his empty cup on the table, he pushed his hands against his knees and rose to a standing position. "Probably a mistake," he thought aloud, "but it's only for a little while—just until they have all the facts of the accident. They might not even call. I gave them your number because I didn't know where I would be staying tonight."

Kirsten attempted to hide her unease. "I thought you were staying in Portland."

"That was my original plan."

She lifted a dubious brow. "Then you still intend to drive inland?"

"I'll go down to Newport—see if the road is passable to Salem or Corvallis."

"And if it's not?"

"I'll stay in Newport." He leaned against the warm bricks of the fireplace and his thumb rubbed pensively along the hard line of his jaw. He seemed to be tossing a weighty decision over in his mind. "There's another reason I came here," he admitted reluctantly.

"Which is?"

"First of all, because I owed you an apology. I

really had no right coming here and trying to get information from you." He shook his head and ran his tense fingers through the thick strands of his coffee-colored hair. "It's just that this case has me beating my head against a brick wall. No one seems to be leveling with me!"

Kirsten didn't respond, content to let him vent his frustration. She realized that she was witnessing a very personal side of Dane which he usually kept restrained.

He slammed his fist against the warm bricks before regaining his composure. "Another reason I came back," he conceded, "was that I wanted to see you again. I needed to know that you were still here—"

"I don't understand."

He smiled bitterly. "I don't blame you. I'm not sure I understand it myself." He drew in a long, ragged breath. "Something happened to me once. I lost someone very close to me. And while I was there at the site of the accident tonight, I had this feeling . . ." He shrugged as if suddenly embarrassed. "I just wanted to make sure that you were okay."

Kirsten shifted in the chair, unconsciously letting her robe gape open to expose the provocative curve of her knee protruding seductively against the plush fabric. Dane's intense gaze dropped to the slim leg before returning to her curious green eyes.

"I appreciate your concern," she said, disregarding the fact that her breathing had become uneven under his seductive stare. "But I've spent enough time at the coast to know how to weather an occasional storm." She smiled nervously and turned to gaze at the fire. The intimacy of the situation was unnerving her and she had trouble finding her voice. "I don't think you should spend any time worrying about me."

"If it were only that easy," he muttered before rolling his eyes to the exposed beams of the pine ceiling.

Her heart went out to him. The accident had brought back all of his painful memories about his dead wife and child. And now he was insinuating that he cared for her. She shook her head and caught her lower lip between her teeth. "Dane," she whispered, "you and I . . . we can't let this happen. It's no good for either of us."

"I've been telling myself that for several weeks," he said, "but I just haven't been able to convince myself." He witnessed the hesitancy in her gaze and knew that she was wavering. Her green eyes had become unsure and inviting. Firelight caught in her hair, streaking the honey-brown strands with gold.

"I made some chowder," she offered, hoping to dissipate the seductive atmosphere in the suddenly intimate room.

"I'm not hungry." His intense eyes bored into hers and she felt her heart miss a beat. She was going to lose everything to this man. She knew it in one breathless instant.

The telephone rang sharply to break the sensual spell. Kirsten was relieved for an excuse to look away from the questions in Dane's eyes. She rose from the chair gracefully and hurried to answer the call. A rough male voice on the other end of the line identified himself as Officer Cooney of the state police and asked to speak to Dane.

Before Kirsten could call to him, Dane was at her side and took the receiver from her hand. The conversation was extremely one-sided, and only on a few occasions did Dane interrupt the officer. Kirsten returned to her position on the couch and slowly sipped the remainder of her wine. The Chablis had become warm but holding the glass in her trembling fingers and sipping the clear liquid helped hide her unease. Being alone with Dane in the middle of the night was disturbing. Though she wanted nothing more than to spend the rest of the night with him, she couldn't allow herself to forget that he was a lawyer for the defense.

Just the realization that she had feelings for Dane made her uncomfortable. She hadn't been intimate with a man since her divorce. Nor had she wanted to. She had considered the fact that she might not ever meet a man whom she would desire, and she hadn't been concerned at the thought. The last thing she wanted in her life was a man. And yet, here she was, thinking about spending the night with the one man who could crucify her.

Slowly Dane replaced the receiver. His jaw had hardened and his thick black brows had pulled together. Wearily, he rubbed the tension from the back of his neck before sinking into the soft cushions of the couch. "She didn't make it," he murmured.

Kirsten swallowed with difficulty. "What about the boy?"

"He's all right. His dad is with him."

Seeing the angry pain on his face pierced Kirsten's heart. "Dane," she whispered. "I'm sorry."

"It's not your fault, Kirsten." He let out a deep breath. "I don't know why I'm taking it so hard."

"Because it reminds you of losing your wife and son," Kirsten said softly.

The skin over Dane's features tightened and his lips drew into a thin line against the injustice of life. "I suppose you're right," he conceded regretfully. "Doesn't matter anyway."

"Of course it does."

"Look, Kirsten, nothing's going to bring them back!" Dane snapped, the anger of six agonizing years resurfacing. He noticed her wince under the assault of his words. "I'm sorry," he apologized.

"It's okay—"

"No, it's not. I had no right to take it out on you. The last few days have been rough, but that's not your problem." He gazed into her eyes and wondered at the bewitching mystery of Kirsten McQueen. The way she looked at him made his blood begin to boil with a passion he had once thought dead. The ache he felt for her made him push his hands deeply into the pockets of his cords. "I think I'd better go," he said huskily. His eyes wandered down the seductive column of her throat, past her collarbones to the swell of her breasts hidden by the cream-colored robe.

"Then you still think you can make it to Portland tonight?" Her heart was pounding erratically in her rib cage. His gaze roved restlessly over her and she found it difficult to smile. Running nervous fingers through her light brown hair, she was conscious only of his compelling scrutiny.

"I think I should try." He took a step closer to her and Kirsten was held by the promises in his eyes.

"But the storm—"

"Kirsten, if I stay here any longer, I don't know if I'll be able to leave." He touched her shoulder. The soft fabric of the robe was familiar and evoked memories of a happier time in his life.

"It's just that . . ."

"What?" he asked, his voice low and commanding. Kirsten felt a shudder of anticipation skitter down her spine.

"It's already late—after midnight."

He stepped closer and his free hand traced the graceful angle of her jaw. She was forced to swallow and close her eyes as his finger moved slowly down her neck, along the collar of the robe, to rest between her breasts, just above her waist, where the downy garment was tied. "I want to stay with you," he admitted, his voice thick, "more than anything I've wanted in a very long time. But it has to be because you want me here."

Her head fell forward with the weight of her decision. She held her forehead in one hand and avoided looking into the desire in his eyes. The warmth of his one finger lingered against her skin and argued with the logic in her mind.

"Look at me," he whispered. She raised her eyes to meet his probing gaze and couldn't hide the tears of frustration that had begun to form behind her eyelids.

"There's just so much more than the two of us," she murmured.

"That's why I think it would be best if I left—now—before we did anything we might regret."

"If it weren't for the lawsuit . . ."

"I never would have met you." The passion in his gaze had deepened. The intense hue was neither gold nor brown, but an erotic hazel. "Thank God for that damned lawsuit."

"This is very hard for me," she whispered.

"It's hard for both of us."

"Oh, Dane—"

"The hell with it," he muttered as the tension of the long night exploded. His free arm wrapped around her waist to pull her body fast against him. She felt the fever of his rapid breathing. His muscles tensed as his arms embraced her and his head lowered to allow his lips to capture hers. His kiss was bold, impatient, as if too many hours of frustration had ignited his smoldering passion.

Her breasts, where they crushed against him, ached for his touch. Ignoring the doubts lingering in her mind, she returned the ardor of his kiss and wound her arms around his neck. Her fingers twined in the thick, dark strands of his hair, and she ignored the fact that what she was surrendering to bordered on insanity.

One strong hand splayed against the small of her back, gently rubbing the soft fabric of her robe against her skin. His other hand caught in her golden brown curls and pulled her head backward, forcing her to stare into the seductive power of his hazel gaze.

"Tell me you want me to stay," he commanded.

"You know I do."

"Despite the circumstances?" he asked softly.

Kirsten knew that he was offering her one last chance to refuse him, giving her one final avenue of escape. "I'm thirty-five years old," she replied, "and I hope I understand myself well enough to know what I want."

"This is important to me," he murmured against her neck, holding her so tightly that she could scarcely breathe. "But you have to realize that it won't affect the way I defend KPSC. What happens tonight between us has nothing to do with what will take place in court."

"I wouldn't expect it to," she whispered.

"Then let me love you tonight," he pleaded as his lips brushed against hers. She responded by cradling his head in her hands and sighing against him. The invitation of her open lips sent a shudder of anticipation through his strained muscles.

His fingers found the knot of velour that held the

creamy fabric together. Slowly it loosened. The robe parted to reveal an enticing glimpse of her body.

"You're beautiful," he whispered hoarsely as his eyes stole down the seductive slit in the garment. Her skin was flushed and the dusky hollow between her breasts invited his touch. His fingers probed beneath the soft fabric to inch up her rib cage before lightly touching one swollen breast.

Kirsten closed her eyes and let her head fall backward, exposing more of her throat to him. He pushed her hair aside and let his lips caress the soft shell of her ear while his hands accepted the weight of her breasts. Her heartbeat was lost in the wild fury of the night. It pounded as erratically as the angry waves against the sand.

She felt alternate currents of searing heat and arctic cold race through her veins. Thoughts of denial had long since escaped her, and she was conscious only of the seductive magic his hands inspired.

His finger moved slowly upward, past the swell of her breasts to her shoulders. Without hurry, as if he had all the time in the world, he gently pushed the robe off her shoulders and it fell to the floor in a puddle of plush ivory.

Kirsten stood before Dane, stripped naked except for her lace panties. He stared into her eyes before dropping to one knee and pressing moist lips to her skin. His hands pressed firmly against the small of her back while his lips caressed the soft skin near her breast.

Her knees started to give way, but he held her upright and slowly opened his mouth against one straining nipple. She moaned at the bittersweet agony his lips created against her soft flesh. "Dear God," she whispered, her fingers running through the wet strands of his hair.

All of his muscles flexed as he gently lowered her to the jade green carpet. Beads of sweat, evidence of the restraint he placed on himself, dotted his forehead. He moved away from her long enough to remove his clothes and toss them aside. Her eyes wandered down the solid length of his body. Lean muscles, looking as if they were oiled because of his sweat, gleamed in the firelight.

"Make love to me," he pleaded, pulling her against him. She felt his legs rubbing against hers. His fingers pressed against the naked length of her spine, pushing her against the hard desire straining in each of his corded muscles. "I've wanted you for so long . . . so long."

As if unable to restrain himself any longer, he removed the one small barrier of her underwear and slowly positioned himself over her. His hands trembled as they smoothed her hair away from her face and he kissed her quivering lips. His eyes had turned as dark as the night and he squeezed them tightly shut as he moved over her.

Her breathing was rapid and shallow with anticipation. Every nerve in her body wanted to be touched by this man with the powerful gaze. She felt the moment of their union, the power of his possession, and began to move in the sure rhythmic strokes he inspired.

Her fingers dug into the solid muscles of his shoulders as the tempo increased and the hot pressure within her swelled to burst in a rush of desperation and need.

"Dane . . ." she cried into the night just as his

answering shudder announced his surrender. His body stiffened before falling against hers in satiation.

Tears of relief and fear pooled in her eyes before sliding down her face. His thumb caressed her cheek but stopped its gentle caress when he realized she was crying.

He reached for a blanket sitting on the edge of the couch and gently covered her body. "Shhh . . ." he whispered. "Everything will be all right. I promise."

"Just hold me," she murmured.

"I will, sweet Kirsten." His arms wrapped securely and possessively over her body. "Forever."

Chapter Seven

$\mathcal{K}$ irsten awakened to the inviting smell of freshly perked coffee. She raised a wary eyelid as unfamiliar noises disturbed her subconscious.

She was alone in the bed. The only evidence that Dane had spent the night with her was the impression still visible on the pillow near hers. She smiled and stretched. Vivid images of the night filled her mind and she realized that she was falling hopelessly in love with the seductive stranger from New York.

Why Dane? Of all the men in the world, why did it have to be Dane Ferguson who attracted her? For all she knew, she was just another in a long line of conquests. Worse yet, perhaps his seduction had been planned, a neatly staged scenario to break down her defenses.

"Stop it," she muttered angrily to herself. "What's done is done." She propped up on one elbow and surveyed the small bedroom. The dim light of dawn filtered into the room through the open weave of the airy draperies.

Her velour robe was lying on the foot of the bed. Kirsten smiled to herself when she saw it. Dane must have retrieved it from the living room and placed it on the bed this morning. That simple, thoughtful act touched her.

Approaching footsteps scraped against the hardwood floor and Kirsten smiled to herself. Holding the sheet over her breasts, she turned her eyes to the doorway.

He paused at the entrance to the room and his severe gaze yielded as he looked down at her slim form. Her hair framed her elegant face in tangled disarray. Green eyes, still seductive from recent slumber, peeked through thick dark lashes. She stretched and the sheet draped across her body molded to her slender figure.

Dane seemed more relaxed this morning, Kirsten decided as she met the invitation in his unguarded stare. The lines of strain around his mouth and eyes had gentled perceptibly. He was dressed in the same cords and sweater he had worn the night before, and his chin was darkened by the morning shadow of his beard. His lean muscles moved fluidly beneath his clothes.

It could be dangerously easy to wake up each morning in Dane's arms, Kirsten thought to herself as an enigmatic smile curved her full lips.

Crossing his arms over his chest, Dane continued to stand in the open doorway. He propped one shoulder against the wooden frame of the door and leaned insolently against it as he regarded Kirsten with his penetrating, deepset eyes.

"I thought I heard sounds of life in here," he

teased, reluctantly dragging his eyes from the seductive swell of her breast hidden beneath the crisp blue sheet up to her eyes.

Although she felt at an incredible disadvantage, lying naked between the sheets, she managed to return his engaging smile and ran her fingers through the tangles in her hair. She tried not to yawn and failed. "Have you been awake long?"

He shrugged his shoulders indifferently. "About an hour, I'd guess."

Kirsten's eyes swept to the digital display on her clock-radio. "But it's barely six—"

"Not in New York."

The statement settled like lead in the intimate room. Words caught in Kirsten's throat. "You're going back, aren't you?" she asked quietly. The fingers clutching the sheet to her breast tensed, twisting the pale blue fabric.

His smile turned wistful and his shoulders slumped slightly. "I have to."

"Do you?" The look of disbelief in her cool green eyes challenged him.

"I've got a practice in New York."

"Of course you do. How could I forget?"

The minute the words were out, Kirsten regretted them. Every muscle in his body had stiffened in defense of her verbal assault.

"I hope you know that last night had nothing to do with your case against the station."

She took her eyes away from his uncompromising stare. "I'd like to believe that," she admitted in a rough whisper.

"Then just trust me."

She lifted a doubtful brow when she turned to face him again. "It's difficult for me."

"Why?"

"Maybe it's because all my life I've had to be wary of soft-spoken, smooth, manipulative men who would like to use me to get what they want."

"Like me?" he asked, the muscles in his arms flexing against his chest.

"Like you."

"Oh, lady." He sighed, looking up at the ceiling. "What have I done to you?" His eyes were shadowed in a self-reproachful pain.

Her heart twisted wretchedly. "Nothing I didn't want," she murmured. "Look, I'm sorry—I didn't mean to get so angry."

"It's just your nature?"

Her green eyes sparkled until she realized that he was teasing. "Call it a character flaw," she muttered with a self-mocking grin. "It seems to come to the surface every time I'm around a man who would like to crucify me on the witness stand."

"That's hitting below the belt, Kirsten," he cautioned.

She shook her golden-brown hair. "No, that's telling it like it is, counselor." Before he could argue, she reached for her robe and slipped it over her shoulders.

He watched her precise movements and caught a provocative glimpse of her slim body as she put her arms through the sleeves, stood, knotted the belt and lifted her thick hair out of the collar of the robe. "Can I buy you breakfast?" she asked, hoping to hide the feeling of desperation growing within her. Dane was leaving! It was only a matter of time before he would disappear from her life only to resurface for a fleeting and heart-wrenching moment at the trial.

She attempted to walk past him, but strong fingers

wrapped over the crook in her arm and held her fast. His chin had hardened and the rage in his eyes became deadly. "Are you trying to say that you regret what happened last night?"

The smile she tried to force trembled. "Regret is too harsh a word," she allowed. "I just think that I wasn't being very rational last night . . . and I hope that I never make that mistake again."

"Mistake?"

"Look, Dane, there's no point in arguing about what happened. I can't deny that what we shared was incredible. I'm just saying that it won't happen again . . . at least not until the court battle is resolved."

His dark eyes narrowed. "And when it is, what then? Do you honestly think that we'll be able to pick up where we left off—just as if the trial hadn't occurred?"

"No." She shook her head sadly and her slim shoulders sagged with an unfair burden. "No, I don't."

"Then what you're saying is that it's over," he deduced aloud.

"I'm saying it never began," she whispered.

The fingers around her arm slackened and Dane's hands clenched in frustration before making a disgusted sound in the back of his throat. "This is your choice, you know."

"Precisely my point. We don't have a choice, Dane."

He strode into the living room and picked up his suitcase before turning to face her. When he did, all trace of emotion had left his intense hazel eyes. "I think I'd better go," he stated as he picked up his Windbreaker from the back of the couch. His eyes swept the top of a nearby table. Just as he reached for his keys, he noticed the newspaper article lying on the coffee table.

He paused as his eyes scanned the newsprint. Kirsten's breath caught in her throat. When Dane stood, he tossed the jacket casually over his arm, pocketed the keys and picked up the article. "Ginevra," he muttered softly, as if to himself. But he wanted a response. He expected one. She could read the unasked questions in his wary gaze.

Kirsten's spine stiffened and the smile she forced to her face was frail. "That's right."

"The proposed nuclear site?"

"Yes."

"You're still interested in it. Why?" He studied every movement on her face, looking for the slightest trace of emotion. Obviously Ginevra meant more to her than she had intoned during the deposition in Lloyd Grady's office.

"I free-lance. Anytime I read something that interests me, something I might do an article on later, I clip it from the paper and put it in my research file." She nervously ran her fingers along the belt of her robe. "I still have to make a living, you know."

Dane felt as if he had inadvertently stumbled onto something important. Kirsten was trying too hard to convince him that Ginevra meant nothing significant. From his years of practice reading people and attempting to make them say what he wanted to hear, Dane understood that Ginevra was somehow involved in the suit against KPSC. The first time the site had been mentioned, in Lloyd Grady's office, a look of caution had crossed the blond attorney's features. Kirsten had caught Lloyd's warning glance and had sidestepped the issue. Ginevra might be the key to the whole damned suit!

"And you're thinking about doing a story on Ginevra?" he prodded.

Dane assumed the same casual manner he had used in the depositions, and Kirsten realized that he was once again the attorney for the defense. Kirsten's heart bled when she knew that what she had feared was true: Dane had come to her seeking a hole in her story, a crack in the suit against KPSC.

Kirsten raised her palms indecisively to the ceiling. "Who knows? Maybe someday."

Dane dropped the subject. Pushing her any further wouldn't get him anywhere. He knew just how hard to press a person and when it was tactful to stop. He'd extracted all the information from her that she would give him. The satisfaction he should have felt in discovering her weakness was painfully absent. "I'll see you later," he stated, returning the clipping to the table and rotating once again toward the door.

"In court, counselor," she returned with a bitter smile.

"If that's the way you want it," he whispered.

"There's no other way. You know it as well as I do."

Without a smile or a regretful look over his shoulder Dane walked to the door, opened it, paused as if he thought better of his movements and then walked out of the house . . . and out of Kirsten's life.

"You're a damned fool," she told herself as she closed the door behind him and slumped against the wall.

A walk along the beach didn't satisfy her, not did it soothe her raw nerves. Evidence of last night's storm only served to remind her of Dane and the short romance they had shared together. The broken shells, tangled seaweed and discarded pieces of driftwood were scattered on the wet sand like pieces of her shattered life.

How could one man affect her so deeply? Kirsten huddled against the damp fog and pushed her hands deep into the pockets of her jacket as she stared out to sea. The gray waters of the Pacific lapped gently on the sand. Why had she let Dane into her heart? He could only destroy her.

Pursing her lips in determination, she forced herself to stand and abandon her post on the exposed rock near the tide pools. Whether she liked the thought or not, it was time to face the music and call Lloyd Grady. If she expected to win her fight against KPSC, her attorney would have to know everything about her conversations with Dane.

Bracing herself against the verbal attack she was sure to get from Lloyd, she mounted the stairs and walked back into the cabin. After discarding her shoes and jacket, she dialed Lloyd's office and after a brief wait was put through to her attorney.

"Kirsten!" He sounded relieved.

"I thought I should call and let you know that you were right," she said.

"About what?"

"Dane Ferguson showed up."

There was a pause in the conversation. "I knew it! That miserable bastard," Lloyd muttered. "I hope you sent him packing."

Kirsten hesitated. "He left, but we talked for quite a while."

"Dear God, Kirsten, what do you mean, quite a while? Ten minutes? An hour? What?"

"I think it ended up to be several hours," Kirsten admitted with a frown. "I thought that maybe I could get some information out of him."

"And did you?" Lloyd asked, unable to hide his disgust.

"Not much . . ."

"Of course not! He's slick, Kirsten, and he's got the reputation to prove it. We're not talking about some two-bit penny-ante kid who's still wet behind the ears, for God's sake! He's one of the best Manhattan has to offer. His fee alone would choke a horse!"

"I know that."

"But you still talked to him." Lloyd let out a tired breath of air. "Damn it, Kirsten, what do you expect me to do? I can't win this suit for you unless you cooperate—with me, not with the defense! You have to remember that Dane Ferguson has only one objective in mind: to win this suit as fast as he can, by any means possible. You're not going to con him the way you conned Fletcher Ross."

Kirsten's anger snapped. "I didn't con Ross, Lloyd. I won the case because I was right! Remember?"

"And you didn't do it by handing over the defense any information I didn't know about."

"Okay, look, I'm sorry."

Lloyd's voice softened. "All right. There's no reason to panic about it. It's over. Just please, be careful, Kirsten. Don't make this kind of mistake again. What Ferguson's done is unethical, but there's not a whole lot we can do except make the best out of a bad situation. Why don't you tell me what you discussed?"

Kirsten repeated her conversations with Dane, excluding the personal aspect and tone. Lloyd listened intently, interrupting her only to clarify a point every now and then.

"It doesn't sound as if he learned anything that he didn't already know," Lloyd stated when Kirsten had finished her dissertation. The Portland attorney sounded relieved, and Kirsten hated to burst his bubble.

"Except for the fact that he found a clipping I'd taken from *The Herald*. It was an article on Ginevra."

"Great," Lloyd muttered. "I'd hate to see him open that can of worms. . . ." He sighed audibly as he collected his thoughts. "Did he read the article?"

"Most of it."

"Did he ask about it?"

"Uh-huh. I told him that I was going to put it in my research file for an article I might write at a later date."

"Did he believe you?"

"I think so. After all, it's the truth."

"Okay, so we got lucky. Look, I don't want you to so much as look at Dane Ferguson when I'm not around. Anytime he wants to see you, tell him it's strictly by the book. Your attorney will have to be present." There was an edge to Lloyd's words, as if he were affronted that Dane had managed to see Kirsten alone. Kirsten sensed that it wasn't just because of the lawsuit.

"I don't think we'll have to worry about that," Kirsten replied. "He was planning to go back to New York."

"When?"

"I don't know. . . . I didn't ask."

"It doesn't matter. In the future, just use your head. You can't expect me to win this for you if you don't cooperate. And try to keep your perspective on this case. If you blow this, you'll lose that two-hundred-thousand-dollar award."

"It's not the money, Lloyd. You know that. I just want to see that justice is served. KPSC had no right to treat me the way they did, and I hope that I can win this suit in order that other women like me won't have to put up with what I did."

"Then for Pete's sake, Kirsten, try to remember who's on your side and who's against you!"

"I will, Lloyd."

"Good."

"Talk to you later."

"And tell me if Ferguson tries to see you again."

Kirsten hung up the phone and went into the kitchen to pour herself a cup of coffee. The morning newspaper was still on the kitchen table, opened to the page Dane had been reading. Kirsten took a sip of the coffee and read the column that had held Dane's interest. It was an article about the previous night's accident.

An image of Dane with mud streaked across his cheek and rain glistening in his hair filled Kirsten's mind. Witnessing that accident had been hard on him. She had read it in the pain in his eyes and the tension of his jaw.

"If only things were different," she whispered, remembering the ecstasy of their lovemaking. "Maybe I could ease your pain . . . make you forget, just for a little while." Then, realizing that she had been daydreaming, she refolded the newspaper and poured her cold coffee down the sink.

The less she thought about Dane the better. Perhaps this morning was a good time to tackle the article about the timber sales slump. She walked back to the living room and sat down at the antique sewing machine on which her typewriter rested.

She tugged off the plastic cover and stared at the

blank page rolled over the carriage. "This isn't going to be easy," she told herself as she placed her hands over the keys. "But somehow you've got to get Dane Ferguson out of your mind."

With new resolve she tackled the job ahead of her, and it wasn't until she paused in her work and rubbed the tension out of her shoulders that she saw the blanket folded on the corner of the couch.

Kirsten's throat went suddenly dry. She stared at the faded quilt and her lower lip trembled. The memory of Dane placing that blanket tenderly over her body last night while murmuring words of love into her ear wouldn't leave her, and she had to fight the tears beginning to sting her eyes.

Chapter Eight

$\mathscr{D}$ane was impatient. He stared out the small window of Fletcher Ross's office and studied the gray skies shadowing the city.

Since leaving Kirsten, Dane had been uneasy. Listening to Fletcher Ross hadn't helped matters. Dane tapped his pencil angrily on the corner of Ross's oversized desk and tried to look pleased while being introduced to Aaron Becker, station manager for KPSC.

"Good to meet you," Becker stated as Dane rose from his chair to accept the station manager's handshake. The short man pumped Dane's hand several times before releasing it. As Becker dropped into the leather couch, he smiled at Dane. The grin was practiced and friendly. Dane didn't trust it for a minute.

"What can I do for you?" Aaron Becker asked pleasantly before he cocked his wrist and pointedly checked the time. He was a busy man. The seconds of his life weren't idly given.

"I just want to ask you a few questions about Kirsten McQueen's employment at KPSC," Dane suggested in an even, professional tone.

Becker responded. If there was anything he respected in a man, it was professionalism. "What do you want to know?" He leaned forward on the expensive couch, hiked his pants up and placed his clasped hands over his knees.

Dane studied the man. Becker was nervous, either by nature or because of added stress. Maybe a combination of the two. "This isn't a deposition, you understand. I'm just trying to clarify a few points in the McQueen case."

"Good."

"How would you describe Ms. McQueen's attitude?" Dane asked the station manager.

"Toward me?"

Dane's dark brows rose slightly. "I was talking in generalities, but, since you brought it up, let's start with her relationship with you. How did Ms. McQueen react to you?"

Becker pulled an exaggerated frown. "Hard to say," he responded, tugging at the knot in his tie. "In the beginning we got along—you are talking about how she handled her work load, right?"

"What do you mean?" Dane's hazel eyes darkened.

"You're not asking about how she reacted to me as a man, are you?"

Dane smiled tightly and his fingers clenched around the pencil before he put it on the desk. "Did she? React to you as a man, I mean."

Becker grinned collusively at Fletcher Ross. The

round attorney squirmed and wiped the sweat from his brow with his handkerchief. "Well, she didn't actually come on to me, if that's what you mean."

"But," Dane prodded, concealing his rage by leaning back in the chair and crossing his arms over his chest.

"But . . . you know how it is. A guy can feel when a woman's hot for him."

"You got that feeling with Kirsten McQueen?" Savage eyes drilled into Aaron Becker, but the anger in Dane's gaze was lost on him.

Becker shrugged uncomfortably. "Yeah, a couple of times. She went through a bad divorce and, well, I could tell she was interested."

"But you didn't pursue a relationship?"

Becker shook his head. The neatly styled hair didn't move. "Naw." He stuck out his lips as if in deep thought. "Probably was a mistake."

"Why do you say that?" Dane's jaw hardened, but he hung onto his façade of civility. The anger flowing through his veins was irrational and would only hinder his quest for the truth.

"Maybe if I would have given her what she wanted, we wouldn't be in this mess today." He laughed aloud. Neither Fletcher Ross nor Dane Ferguson cracked a smile. Dane's face remained impassive. Only the tightening of skin over his cheekbones gave any indication of his restrained emotions.

"So you think that Ms. McQueen's lawsuit was a vendetta aimed at you?"

Becker sobered. "I wouldn't go so far as to say that."

"Then what will you say when you're called to give testimony? Would you swear, under oath, that

Kirsten McQueen was, let's see, how did you phrase it—" Dane eyed his notes. "Here it is. Would you swear that Ms. McQueen was 'hot for you?' "

"Of course not." Becker looked angrily at Fletcher Ross. "Hey, what is this? Isn't this guy on our side?"

Fletcher Ross raised his broad shoulders and with a shake of his head indicated to Aaron that he understood nothing about the New Yorker's tactics.

"I'm trying to defend KPSC," Dane pointed out, leaning over the desk. "And in order to do that I would like to understand Kirsten McQueen's motives for the lawsuit."

"You think I could understand that woman? No way!"

"But didn't you just say that you could feel that she was interested in you as a man?"

"That's different than reading her mind, for crying out loud!"

"Is it?"

Becker's face had flushed scarlet and his fingers drummed nervously on his knee. His full lips pulled into an introspective pout. "Just what is it you want to know?"

Dane forced a congenial smile onto his face. "I just want to know why Kirsten McQueen initiated the suit, an age-discrimination suit, against KPSC."

"I don't know." Aaron Becker looked from Fletcher Ross to Dane Ferguson. "I suppose she doesn't think she got a fair shake. She probably feels that she didn't deserve to get canned."

"Did she?"

Becker rose from his chair and began pacing restlessly in front of the desk. "She was getting pushy. She started demanding things I couldn't give her. She wanted to cover national stories and I was happy with the man I had covering national news. Then, she"—he paused as if carefully considering his words —"she wanted to do more investigative stories in and about Oregon. The whole idea would have thrown off our format. I told her no."

"How did she react?" Dane pressed his elbows on the desk and cradled his chin in his hands as he studied Aaron Becker. The grandstanding was over and the station manager was finally cooperating, or so it appeared.

Becker snorted in disgust. "Like any emotional woman. She flew off the handle."

"In your office."

"Right."

"Were there any other witnesses to her emotional outburst?"

"I can't remember—didn't I answer these questions during the last trial?"

"Some of them," Dane conceded. "So you fired Ms. McQueen and you think she filed the lawsuit in retaliation."

"Yeah, I guess so. Something like that."

"Did you?" Dane demanded, his voice stone cold.

"What do you take me for, an idiot? If Kirsten McQueen had kept her nose clean, she'd still have a job at the station. She was getting to be more trouble than she was worth."

"So you used her argument with you as the excuse to fire her."

"I didn't need an excuse. She gave me reasons. Good reasons. It's all in her personnel file. Don't you have it?"

Dane's gaze remained cool when he leveled it on the hostile station manager. "I've got it. I'd just like to hear your impressions of the situation."

"Well, as far as I'm concerned, Kirsten McQueen is a real pain in the backside. She was trouble all along."

"Not according to the employee records," Dane observed.

Becker waved off Dane's remark with a flip of his wrist. "Yeah, well, I tried to give her the benefit of the doubt. Seems like that might have been a mistake." Once again the short man glanced at his watch.

"Back to the argument," Dane said, pressing the eraser of the pencil he had picked up to his lips and ignoring Becker's obvious ploy to end the discussion.

"The last argument with Kirsten?"

Dane winced at Becker's familiar use of her name. It soured Dane's stomach to think that anyone as slippery as Aaron Becker would know Kirsten personally. "Right. You stated that she was interested in doing more in-depth stories." Becker nodded. "Like what? Can you give me an example?"

Aaron tossed up his hand as if the question were irrelevant. "It didn't matter—anything slightly controversial."

Dane's hazel eyes fixed on Becker's smug face. "Such as Ginevra?" he asked.

The station manager blanched and shot Fletcher Ross a glance of fear before recovering himself. "That was something she was interested in," Becker conceded. "She also had her eye on an alleged drug ring and asked to do a report on one of the state senators who got himself into a little trouble in Salem. . . . There were a lot of stories she wanted to check into. Unfortunately for her, we didn't have the time or the money to finance some of her half-baked ideas."

Fletcher Ross hoisted his large frame out of his chair as if to end the discussion.

Dane wouldn't let go. "Wait a minute. You run a news program. Don't you cover all the news?" Becker's story wasn't adding up.

Aaron impatiently transferred his weight from one foot to the other. "The type of story Kirsten McQueen wanted to report was the flashiest, trashiest scandal to hit the streets. In my opinion, Kirsten was more interested in gossip than news. And that kind of reporting isn't compatible with the way I run my station. KPSC has a responsibility to its viewers and a reputation in the community.

"Now, unless you have any other questions, I've really got to get back to the station."

Dane nodded curtly and Aaron Becker strode hastily out of the tension-filled office.

"Need a ride to the airport?" Fletcher Ross asked, and Dane was forced to smile at the Portland attorney's tactless way of getting rid of him.

"No thanks. I asked your secretary to call me a cab the minute she saw Aaron Becker leave. It should be here soon." Dane snapped his briefcase closed and noticed the relief in Ross's dark eyes. Having Dane Ferguson set up camp in his office made the Portland attorney nervous.

"Is there anything I can do for you while you're in Manhattan?" Ross asked, hoping to look sincere.

"Pray," Dane suggested unkindly. "Unless I start getting some straight answers, we're going to need all the help we can get."

The portly man seemed surprised. "You think Aaron Becker lied to you?"

"Let's just say that I think he may have exaggerated a little," Dane replied as he looked out the window and saw a cab pull up to the curb near Ross's office.

Tossing his raincoat over his arm, Dane grabbed his briefcase and started toward the door.

"You'll keep me posted, let me know how you're progressing?" Ross asked uncomfortably. "And if I can be of any assistance—"

Dane flashed the Portland attorney his most disarming grin. "You'll be the first to know." With his final words he walked through the small maze of interlocking offices, pushed open the door and stepped into the cold Portland rain.

Kirsten dropped the manila envelope into the appropriate slot at the post office. She knew it wasn't her most eloquent piece of journalism, but the article on the timber sales slump was precise and to the point— exactly what the editor of *Update* magazine had requested. With any luck, the magazine would buy the article and show some interest in the other ideas she had submitted with the article.

The post office was located in the business section of Newport and the offices of *The Herald* were only a few blocks east. Kirsten decided to talk to the reporter who had written the story on Ginevra. It took only a short time to walk to the brightly painted cabin that had been converted into official headquarters of the newspaper.

"May I help you?" a pert redhead with an upturned nose and easy smile asked as Kirsten entered the building.

"I'm looking for Laura Snyder," Kirsten said, returning the young woman's friendly grin and wiping away the drops of rain that still clung to her flushed cheeks. The weather had turned cool again. "I don't have an appointment."

The redhead beamed. "I doubt if you'll need one. You're Kirsten McQueen, aren't you?"

"That's right. . . ."

The receptionist extended her hand. "I'm Peggy Monteith. You're something of a legend around here, you know."

"A legend?" Kirsten took the young woman's hand, but the twinkle in her eye indicated that she thought the idea amusing and unjustified. "I don't think—"

Peggy waved off Kirsten's modesty with a flip of her wrist. "Don't give me that. It took a lot of guts for you to stand up to that television station the way you did. Around here, and probably throughout the entire state, you've become a local hero . . . or heroine."

"Were you looking for me?" another female voice asked. Kirsten turned to face a petite woman whose only indication of her age was the slight smattering of gray in her short black hair. "I'm Laura Snyder. I heard most of the conversation from my desk." Laura cocked her head in the direction of a thin partition. "There's not a whole lot of privacy in this office."

Kirsten offered her hand and Laura shook it. "I'd like to talk to you for a minute about an article you wrote. It was in the paper a couple of days ago," she explained.

"And I thought you were going to offer me an exclusive interview with the woman who stood up to KPSC and won."

Kirsten smiled wistfully. "Not yet," she admitted. "The station appealed. It looks as if my victory might be short-lived."

"So I heard." Laura crossed her arms over her chest and studied Kirsten carefully as she leaned against the corner of Peggy's desk. "But that's certainly no reason to think that you won't win the appeal. The way I understand it, you did a pretty good job of proving that the station discriminated against you."

"I'll have to give that credit to my attorney," Kirsten ventured. "He's the reason I won."

"He's still on your side, isn't he?"

"So far." Kirsten considered her conversation with Lloyd earlier in the day. He'd come close to withdrawing from the case—or at least he'd wanted her to think so.

"Why don't you come into my office, such as it is?" Laura suggested.

After leading Kirsten to the small area behind the partition and offering her a cup of coffee, Laura took a seat behind her cluttered desk and smiled at the slim woman with the intelligent green eyes. Folding plump hands over an unruly stack of papers, Laura asked, "What can I do for you?"

"I saw your article on Ginevra," Kirsten stated, noting that Laura didn't seem surprised in the slightest when she mentioned the article. It was almost as if Laura had anticipated what Kirsten was about to say. "I thought you might give me some information on what's happening over there."

"That article seems to have caught everyone's attention," Laura replied, shaking her head. "You're not the first person who's asked me about it. There was a man in here this morning. Tall fella. Good-looking man with an eastern accent. Seems he was interested in my article too." Laura's sharp brown eyes were mildly curious.

Kirsten's heart missed a beat and a sinking sensation swept over her. "Don't tell me. The man who was here this morning—his name was Dane Ferguson, wasn't it?"

"None other." Laura pursed her lips and nodded thoughtfully. "He's the hotshot KPSC hired to defend the station, isn't he?"

Kirsten met the friendly reporter's serious gaze. "The same. He'd already seen me earlier this morning —about the case. I didn't know he'd show up here."

"Strange, isn't it?" Laura conjectured with a thoughtful pout. "Why do you think he's interested in Ginevra?"

Kirsten lifted her shoulders. "I don't know, but I suspect it has something to do with my case."

"That's what I thought," Laura agreed.

"Did you ask him?"

"No. I thought I'd learn more from him by just listening to what he had to say."

"Which was?"

"Nothing." Laura's full lips pursed. "But I got the feeling that he wasn't happy about something. He seemed restless, as if he were trying to figure out something he didn't really understand." Her dark eyes warmed. "If you ask me, Kirsten, you've got him running scared."

"I doubt it," Kirsten admitted. "I don't think Mr. Ferguson is the kind to scare easily."

"Maybe you're right. He seemed like the type that would like a challenge." Laura rubbed her temple. "But just think what he's got at stake here. If you win your case against KPSC, he'll never live it down, just like before during the Stone Motor trial. You're just one woman with a grievance in Oregon and he's the best money can buy. He's got a lot to lose."

Noticing Kirsten's whitened pallor and realizing that she was straying from the reason for Kirsten's visit, Laura dismissed the subject with a wave of her plump fingers. "So what do you want to know about Ginevra?"

"Everything, I suppose."

"Don't we all. If we had the answers to that one, there wouldn't be much of a controversy over it, would there?"

"I guess not," Kirsten admitted, glad that the topic of conversation had shifted from Dane Ferguson. "How did you get interested in Ginevra?"

"That's pretty simple," Laura replied. "It's a pretty hot subject around here . . . probably because the location of the site is so close. Anyway, I've got a couple of friends who are in an antinuclear power group, and they asked me to write an article against the site."

"But your article wasn't against it."

"No—I decided to point out both sides of the issue. Needless to say, my friends weren't too happy about it."

"It's not easy to be objective."

"Not on something as controversial as Ginevra," Laura agreed.

"Everything I know about the site was in my article, but if you want some more information, why don't you call June Dellany? She's a friend of mine— or at least she was until my article on Ginevra was published." Laura scribbled a name and telephone number on a small sheet of paper and handed it to Kirsten, who accepted the scrap of paper, stuffed it into her purse and finished her coffee.

"Thanks a lot," Kirsten stated as she rose to leave.

"No trouble at all," Laura replied with a slow-spreading grin. "And just let me know when I can get that interview."

"As soon as my case is decided," Kirsten promised as she left the small building.

Rain poured from the dark sky and the wind caught in her hair, but she didn't notice. Her thoughts had turned inward and her heart twisted in agony. So Dane had been checking on Ginevra. He'd noticed the clipping in her apartment and he'd looked up the source.

Her small fist clenched in anger. Whatever she had shared with Dane had meant nothing to him. He'd seduced her into thinking that he cared for her—if just a little. But when the chips were down, the truth of the matter was that Dane had used her solely to gain information about the trial. The seduction was just part of the plan to discredit her, and she'd been a fool to think otherwise.

At least now I understand, she thought grimly to herself. *The battle lines have been drawn.*

Chapter Nine

Jet lag. Or maybe it was general fatigue. Whatever the reason, Dane was irritable. The unscheduled two-hour layover in Denver hadn't helped matters and probably had contributed to the headache beginning to pound behind his eyes. The trip to Oregon had been a strain, and the worst part of it was that he was little better off now than when he had left New York City three days earlier.

Even the few hours he'd shared with Kirsten had turned against him. He had hoped to get information from her, but instead he had left her with the unlikely feeling that he had just given up the only thing of real value in his life. Discussing the case with her had only added to his misgivings as had his meeting with Fletcher Ross and Aaron Becker. Dane had left Portland with the taste of disgust in his mouth.

It was evident that both Ross and Becker shared Harmon Smith's opinion that Kirsten McQueen was trouble. Dane didn't understand it. Though Aaron Becker had worked with Kirsten for several years, he had claimed that she had been a pain in the rear all along—a direct contradiction to the employee records in the files of KPSC.

Dane walked through the concourse at JFK and threaded his way past other, slower travelers who were making early morning connections in New York. He didn't have any baggage to collect, as he had carried his garment bag onto the plane himself and it was now draped over his shoulder as he pushed his way out of the crowded terminal.

Taxicabs, all a dingy yellow, were idling in wait as he walked out of the building and into the first gray streaks of dawn. After catching the next available cab, he sighed wearily and he braced himself for the ride back to Manhattan.

Relaxation was impossible in the battered Chevy as, without warning, it alternately lurched forward only to slow abruptly, according to the whims of the brooding driver.

Gratefully, the burly man wasn't inclined to make idle conversation at six in the morning, and Dane stared into the half light of dawn toward the winking lights of the heart of New York City. As the sun rose in the sky the lights of Manhattan disappeared and the dark skyline of the city took shape against the backdrop of what promised to be a brilliant summer day.

Dane closed his eyes and leaned his head against the worn cushion of the backseat before pinching the bridge of his nose with his forefinger and thumb. He couldn't shake the feeling that Fletcher Ross and Aaron Becker were covering their tracks in an attempt to pawn Kirsten off as a scapegoat. But for the life of him, Dane couldn't understand their motives.

Kirsten had proved herself to be an intelligent and thoughtful woman. The image Ross and Becker had painted was decidedly less kind. Why?

Dane had suspected that the answer might lie in that proposed nuclear site, but when he'd questioned the reporter who had written the article on Ginevra, he'd come up empty. Again. The whole damned lawsuit was beginning to take on a new and sinister dimension. It was as if people were purposely trying to thwart him in his quest for the truth. But he should have expected it, Dane thought jadedly, his cynicism surfacing.

The cab screeched to a halt in front of Dane's apartment building. It was a modest but comfortable red brick structure on East 72nd Street. Though not luxurious, it served his needs. He had rented the apartment when he had first moved to Manhattan, and now that he could afford a much more expensive place to live, he found himself reluctant to move. He was comfortable where he was and he didn't want to disturb that comfort. A larger place might remind him of a time in his life that he would rather forget. Those happy memories of Sam and Julie had a way of making him incredibly despondent, twisting his brief joy into a melancholy pain that made his life alone seem empty and hollow.

Kirsten McQueen could change all that, he contemplated, and then abruptly changed the course of his thoughts. Until the lawsuit was decided, he had nothing to offer her.

His apartment was on the third floor. He unlocked the door, walked inside and threw his bag over the back of the modern rust-colored couch. Tugging uncomfortably at his tie, he strode over to the bar, splashed three fingers of bourbon into a glass and drank the warm liquor in one swallow.

It was the first time he'd taken a drink in the morning since Julie's death. The liquid hit his stomach and he felt no satisfaction in the sensation—nor in his life, for that matter. Maybe the bustling city wasn't for him. Maybe he belonged on the other side of the continent, where he could make love to a beautiful woman and watch the sun set in a burst of golden flame as it settled into the horizon of the calm Pacific. He considered another drink, and pushed the wayward thought aside.

Raking his fingers through his hair, he walked over to the desk he had pushed into a corner of the living room and reached for the phone. After calling the office and explaining that he wouldn't make it in until early afternoon, he showered, shaved and changed into a clean business suit. He was dog tired, and all he wanted to do was sleep for a solid twenty-four hours.

But he couldn't. The image of Kirsten lingered in his mind and he knew that he wouldn't be able to rest until he'd found a way to defend KPSC. As he snapped his watch onto his wrist, he felt a twinge of guilt. He was torn between his feelings for Kirsten and the obligation of his promise to Harmon Smith. There was no room for any argument; regardless of what had happened between himself and Kirsten McQueen, Dane still owed Harmon Smith a very large debt, one that money couldn't begin to repay.

"Doesn't matter anyway," he reminded himself, remembering the cool manner in which Kirsten had dismissed him yesterday morning.

But why wouldn't anyone give him a straight answer? He tried to tell himself that it really wasn't his concern, that it wasn't so much the truth he wanted, but a perspective on the case. But his most convincing logic couldn't ignore the one obvious fact that everyone involved in this case seemed to be lying through his teeth. Including Kirsten. She hadn't been straight with him about Ginevra—he sensed it.

A cold feeling in the pit of Dane's stomach suggested to him that once before he hadn't been as concerned for the truth as much as he had been in proving his client's innocence. In the end it had cost him much more than his reputation, and he wouldn't let it happen again.

Without any further soul-searching, Dane called Harmon Smith's secretary and made an appointment to see the president of Stateside Broadcasting Corporation later in the day.

"Dane!" Harmon Smith marched across the room and pumped Dane's arm furiously. His smile was genuine, if a little nervous. "Can I get you a drink?" Ignoring the negative sweep of Dane's head, Smith turned to the petite receptionist who had escorted Dane into the room. "Sylvie, pour him a drink, would you?" His watery blue eyes looked upward into Dane's and his forehead wrinkled thoughtfully. "Bourbon, isn't it?"

Rather than risk a useless argument, Dane nodded. "Bourbon's fine," he replied with a slight grimace before accepting the hastily prepared drink.

Harmon Smith's office was as understated and elaborate as his residence. Brass lamps, expensive carpet, solid wood furniture, original oil paintings— the elegant trappings of wealth created an atmosphere of sedate affluence and comfort. The only thing seemingly out of place was Smith himself. The nervous man didn't blend into the complacent luxury.

He took a long sip of his Scotch and water, lit a cigarette and settled into his overstuffed leather chair. The receptionist left the room and he waved Dane into one of the side chairs near the desk.

"So you're back from Oregon, are you? Tell me, how's it going out there?" Smith asked with a worried frown.

"It's coming along," Dane said, taking a sip of his drink and regarding Smith intently. "Not as well as I'd hoped, but the defense is shaping up."

Harmon Smith appeared relieved. "Good," he muttered, taking a drag from his cigarette and letting the smoke filter out through his nose.

"It could be better, though, if I'd get a little more cooperation."

"Cooperation? From whom? What are you talking about? Isn't that bitch talking to you?" Faded blue eyes filled with concern settled on Dane.

A muscle in the back of Dane's jaw began to tighten at the abrasive words, and his back stiffened as if in defense, but he managed to hide his anger. Dane wanted information, and he wouldn't get it by letting the president of Stateside Broadcasting Corporation anger him. The best strategy was to give Harmon Smith enough rope to hang himself—then maybe Dane could get to the bottom of this mess.

"The point is—no one is leveling with me."

Smith's face flushed and his palm slapped the desk. "Why that self-righteous little—"

Dane's hazel eyes blazed. "I'm not talking about Kirsten," Dane interjected. "And I think you'd better get used to calling her Ms. McQueen."

"Why?"

Dane shifted in his chair and regarded Harmon Smith with unforgiving hazel eyes. "It's unlikely you'll be called to testify, but if you are, the last thing we can afford is to have you, or anyone else remotely associated with running KPSC, come on like a vindictive male chauvinist out to get a woman." Smith looked as if he were about to interrupt, but Dane wouldn't allow it. The skin over his features had stretched taut; the corners of his mouth pulled grimly downward. "You'd better face it, Harmon, this is a tough case—one you can't afford to lose. And it's going to be tried on Oregon soil. We're the outsiders. We can't let anything we say rile the jury or prejudice even one member against us."

Harmon settled back in his chair, properly chastised, but still eyeing Dane speculatively. "Since when did you get so scrupulous?"

"Since I had my back pushed into a corner, Harmon. Now, you asked me to take on this case and I have, but we're going to play by my rules—or it'll be a sure bet that we'll lose. Lloyd Grady will see to that personally." He paused for a moment, letting his wrath slowly expire. "Don't forget that this case was already tried once."

"So what's your point?" Harmon grumbled, crushing his cigarette and reaching for another.

"No one is giving me straight answers. And I'm not just talking about the plaintiff."

"What do you mean?" Instantly, Harmon Smith was wary. His lighter clicked open and he paused to light the cigarette clamped between his teeth.

"Don't get me wrong. She hasn't exactly been helpful, and that attorney of hers, Lloyd Grady, isn't letting her say anything that might help our defense."

"You must have expected that, for God's sake." Harmon Smith finished his drink and pushed the empty glass aside.

"What I didn't expect was to find that my associate, Fletcher Ross, and one of my star witnesses, a guy by the name of Aaron Becker, don't want to level with me."

"You think they're lying?" Smith was mildly surprised but definitely not angry.

"I mean that Becker's testimony is inconsistent. And Ross doesn't seem to give a damn. I checked. KPSC's employee records, supposedly created and reviewed by Becker, state one thing; he says another. The discrepancy won't hold water in court."

"I thought you said things were progressing," Smith growled.

"As well as can be expected under the circumstances. But if I want to win this suit, I'm going to have to get a lot more cooperation from everyone out there."

"Including Aaron Becker?"

"And Fletcher Ross."

Harmon Smith stubbed out his cigarette and frowned. His sandy-colored brows rose, wrinkling his forehead. "Don't you think you misread the situation in Portland? What would Fletcher Ross have to gain by lying to you?"

"Beats me."

"He's supposed to be on our side, for Christ's sake—Becker, too, for that matter."

"Then why the secrecy?"

Harmon Smith shook his balding head. "Becker must have been confused. As to Ross, he's probably a little resentful of you. It looks like a slap in the face to have you call the shots on the appeal, since he lost the first battle."

"I think it's more than that." Dane's hazel eyes knifed through Harmon Smith.

"Such as?"

"I think they're covering up for something. Nothing else makes much sense. And I think they're hoping that Kirsten McQueen will take the fall."

"That's ridiculous," Harmon protested.

"Is it?" Dane rubbed his thumb along his chin. "I don't think so."

"I told you why we're so eager to make an example of Ms. McQueen. We just can't let her get away with the lawsuit." Sweat was beginning to collect over Smith's anxious, watery eyes.

"I know, I know—a dangerous precedent, right?"

"Exactly!" Harmon Smith's fingers began drumming distractedly on his desk.

"Then you better tell your boys in Oregon to come clean, Harmon. The only way we'll win this case is to have all the facts and submit them to the jury in a manner beneficial to our defense. The minute we start lying, it's all over." Dane rose, as if to end the interview.

"But you do think we will win, don't you?" Harmon asked, attempting to hide his nervous concern.

"That depends, Harmon. But you can't expect me to work with my hands tied." Dane swung out of the office gritting his teeth. He'd suspected that Smith was aware of Ross's sleazy tactics, and now Dane was certain that Harmon Smith was stonewalling him along with Ross, Becker and everyone else associated with this damned case. An uneasy feeling tightened his stomach into knots, and for a desperate moment he felt trapped, caught in a web of deception he didn't understand.

Dane took the elevator downstairs and was in the lobby of the Stateside Building when he noticed Frank Boswick, Harmon Smith's assistant, hurrying out of the building. He was the one man who had been honest with Dane the first night that Harmon Smith had presented his case. In three swift strides Dane was beside the younger man, and Frank smiled in recognition.

"How are you—Ferguson, isn't it?"

"That's right, and I'm fine," Dane replied. "If you've got a minute, I'd like to talk to you about the McQueen case."

Boswick checked his watch. His smile was lopsided but genuine. "I've got a little time," he admitted.

"Good. How about a cup of coffee?"

Frank Boswick agreed and the two men settled on a busy café a few blocks west of the Stateside Building. The small restaurant was doing a brisk noon business, but Dane was able to spot a table near the back that would afford a modicum of privacy.

The coffee was served by an efficient waitress whose plain face held no sign of expression as she placed the two steaming cups of black liquid on the Formica tabletop.

"What can I do for you?" Frank Boswick asked, taking a sip of the hot coffee and observing Dane over the rim of his cup.

"I hoped you could clear up a few problems I'm having with the McQueen case."

"Problems?" Frank's thick eyebrows shot over the rims of his thick glasses.

"I'm having trouble getting the truth from Fletcher Ross and Aaron Becker for starters—"

"Not to mention Harmon Smith," Frank guessed with a grimace.

Dane nodded patiently. "He hasn't been the most helpful. Yet, he expects me to win when the case comes to trial."

Frank chuckled, but the sound was hollow. "The whole thing's crazy, if you ask me."

"I'm asking. What do you mean? Why can't I get any straight answers? Why is Harmon so insistent that Kirsten McQueen is nothing but a money-grubbing ex-employee with a grudge? He seems to think that she initiated the suit out of spite."

"And you don't think she did?"

"I'm not sure—not until I get all the facts, and so far that hasn't been easy. I can't even count on my associate for any help."

"He's probably not too fond of you. If you win this case, it will only prove what everyone's thinking: that he did a lousy job during the first trial."

"But that's no reason to try to make it harder for me. We're supposed to be working for the same cause." Dane shook his head in frustration and disgust.

Frank stared into his coffee, absorbing all of Dane's words. He checked his watch before finally rubbing his fingers along his cheek and gazing out of the window at the front of the building. "You're right," he agreed. "I don't know why they haven't told you the whole story from the beginning." He shifted uncomfortably in his chair and drained his cup.

"As I understand it," Frank proclaimed, "the controversy over firing Kirsten McQueen started several months before she was actually let go." His dark eyes rose to meet Dane's curious gaze.

Nodding, Dane silently encouraged Harmon

Smith's assistant to continue. "Kirsten had shown more than just a passing interest in a place called Ginevra. It's a site planned for the second nuclear power plant in Oregon."

"I've heard of it."

"Then you know that the construction of another nuclear power facility in the Northwest was subject to a lot of controversy and public interest due to the failed WPPSS, or Whoops as it's called in that part of the country."

"I read something about it."

"To make a long story short, the Washington Public Power Supply System declared that it couldn't repay several billion dollars in bonds sold to the public to construct the project. On top of that, construction was never finished. It was a real fiasco, not only in the Northwest, but across the country. Thousands of investors lost their savings and confidence, and the municipal bond market dropped. Some financial advisers expect that the confidence level will never be the same. The people in the Northwest feel abused and an incredible amount of lawsuits are still unsettled."

Dane knew all about WPPSS, but he listened to Frank and was relieved to find out that someone seemed to be telling him the truth. "So what does this have to do with Kirsten McQueen?" Dane asked, finishing his coffee.

"For some reason that I sure as hell don't understand, Aaron Becker, the station manager for KPSC, didn't want Kirsten on the story. But she was persistent. She wanted more than the usual fluff stories assigned to women reporters at KPSC, and continued to press Becker about Ginevra."

Dane was forced to smile at Frank Boswick's description of the events. He could well imagine the green fire that would spark in her intelligent eyes if Kirsten were told certain stories were out of her league. Tethering her to mild human interest stories would only add fuel to the fire of challenge that burned within her.

"So you think the key to the entire lawsuit is Ginevra?" Dane surmised when he picked up the bill.

Frank shrugged as if he'd given away too many company secrets. "It looks that way to me."

The two men made their way out of the crowded café, shook hands and parted ways.

With renewed conviction Dane decided to return to Oregon. Unfortunately, the trip would have to wait until he'd cleared up a few things at the office. He had several cases that he had to review and couldn't be ignored. He found that thought discouraging.

He turned toward the street and hailed a passing cab. It had been less than forty-eight hours since he'd last seen Kirsten and it already seemed like a lifetime.

Chapter Ten

Two weeks had passed since she had seen or heard from Dane. Each day Kirsten felt a little less pain and a little more anger. Her wrath was aimed for the most part at herself—for letting Dane abuse her, and if she called herself a fool, she decided Dane was worse: a deceptive bastard who had intentionally seduced her in hopes of defaming her.

"You played into his hands," she reminded herself as she straightened the neatly typed pages of her résumé. She chided herself for being so naive. Once before a man had used her and she had sworn it would never happen again. The painful divorce from Kent should have been all the warning she needed about powerful men. Apparently it wasn't.

The telephone rang and the noise made her jump. Each time the damn instrument had rung in the past ten days, she had futilely hoped that it would be Dane. Of course, she had been wrong. Ignoring her racing pulse, she answered the phone on the desk and stared through the window at the blue-gray waters of the ocean.

"Kirsten!" Lloyd's voice rang enthusiastically over the wires when she answered the telephone.

"How are you, Lloyd?"

"Great, just great. Hey, listen, we've got a court date, and barring some unforeseen schedule changes, we'll be facing KPSC on September tenth." Lloyd sounded ready to do battle with the formidable foe.

Kirsten's heart pounded in her chest. The reality of the trial stared her in the face. The expressionless jurors, the judgmental looks of disdain from Fletcher Ross, the interest of hungry reporters—and Dane. With his unforgiving hazel eyes, his smooth Eastern manners, his ingratiating smile and his needle-sharp intent to destroy her character, Dane would crucify her during the trial.

"Is the tenth okay?" Lloyd asked. She could hear the worry in his voice. "Kirsten?"

She closed her eyes to compose herself. If she had any brains at all, she would tell Lloyd what happened between herself and the famous New York attorney. Maybe Lloyd would find a way to force Dane off the case. "The tenth is fine," she managed to say, her words faint.

"You're sure?"

"Of course."

There was a weighty pause in the conversation. "You're not having second thoughts, are you?"

"A little late for that, wouldn't you say?"

"Maybe not. I could suggest an out-of-court settlement," Lloyd proposed.

"No!" Kirsten drew in a steadying breath. "This

suit isn't about dollars and cents, Lloyd, you know that. It's not the money—"

"I know. It's the principle of the thing, right?"

"Right."

"Tell it to the jury."

"I intend to. And I'm sure Ferguson will see to it that they don't believe me." She sighed.

"He's back in Portland, you know."

Kirsten's heart stopped and she had to lean against the wall for support. Dane was back! "No . . . no, I didn't."

"I thought he might have called you."

If only he had! Kirsten couldn't prevent the tears from forming in her eyes. "Why?"

"Because I ran into him—at the courthouse. I think he was waiting for Fletcher Ross. Anyway, I gave him a piece of my mind about talking to you without my presence, told him I might move for a mistrial."

"What did he say?" Kirsten asked breathlessly.

"He called my bluff, told me to go ahead."

"And are you?"

"Of course not. We've waited long enough as it is. Putting off the trial would only weaken our position. Right now, public sentiment is with you, but in six months, who knows? The public isn't known for its loyalty or memory."

"I see."

She heard Lloyd draw in a long breath. "What I hope you see, Kirsten, is that you can't talk to Ferguson, Ross, Becker or any of the lot unless I'm with you. This case is as important to me as it is to you, and I'm warning you not to do anything that might blow it."

"I understand," she whispered, knowing exactly

what Lloyd meant. If Lloyd Grady should win against Dane Ferguson, it would be an important feather in his cap. With the national news coverage, Lloyd's fame in legal circles would be guaranteed and his new prestige would in turn bring him wealthier clients and more interesting cases. This was Lloyd's shot at the big time.

"We both have a lot at stake," Kirsten agreed.

"I'm glad you realize that. For a while I thought that you'd forgotten." His voice was filled with relief. "Then, let's go for it. I'll give you a call if anything comes up. Oh, have you heard any more about the job in San Francisco?"

"Not yet, but I've got my fingers crossed," she replied, her eyes drifting to the résumé stacked on the desktop.

"Good-bye."

Kirsten hung up the receiver with trembling fingers. The tears that had pooled in her eyes began to run down her face. "What am I doing?" she asked herself as she wiped her eyes with her fingertips, but vivid images of Dane assaulted her mind and continued to haunt her. "Why can't I hate him?"

Because I love him, she thought with a wry grimace. *I love him more than any woman should love a man.* Acknowledging this was more of a burden than she could bear and she had to find a way to rid herself of the torturous thoughts of Dane.

Without much enthusiasm she changed into her running shorts, a cotton T-shirt and her Nikes before dashing out of the house. As soon as she descended the weathered steps and her feet hit the beach, she took off, forcing herself to run northward. A cool breeze greeted her, but she bent her head against the wind and established her pace.

The run took nearly an hour and her muscles screamed against the abuse of seven miles when she finally returned to her starting point near the steps and stretched out her aching calves. Her hair was damp, as much from her sweat as the light mist that had begun to settle in the air. The dense gray clouds made it impossible to view the sun, which was probably settling behind the horizon.

Wearily, Kirsten trudged up the stairs, thinking of a hot shower and light dinner. She was exhausted, but at least the cobwebs that had gathered in her mind had disappeared and she could think clearly again.

She stopped her ascent before reaching the top step. Dane was waiting for her on the small landing from which the stairs angled down the cliff face. He stood on the weathered planks and leaned over the rail as he squinted against the wind.

Kirsten's heart twisted with inner agony when she recognized him. His dark hair caught in the wind and his brooding hazel eyes never left hers. Slowly, she finished the climb and silently braced herself against the magnetism in his eyes. Against the most feminine urges within her she told herself she had to avoid him—being with him was far too dangerous.

"What are you doing here?" she asked as she wiped her hands on her shorts and held his steady gaze.

"I came to see you."

"I thought I made myself clear the last time you were here."

"You weren't being honest with me or yourself."

"Look who's talking!" she blurted out.

"Kirsten, let's start over—"

"Forget it. I talked to my attorney. He's threatened to walk off the case if I make the mistake of talking to you without him." She managed to mask the turbulent emotions racing through her with the cool self-assurance she had assumed as an objective reporter in front of the news camera.

"He told me the same thing."

"Did he? Is that why you're here?" Her large green eyes narrowed as she stared up at him. "You'd like that, wouldn't you? If Lloyd dropped my case, it would certainly make it easier for you."

"The case has nothing to do with the reasons I came to see you," he stated, ignoring her taunts and the vibrant green anger sparking in her eyes.

"Save that for someone who'll believe it!"

"You believe it, Kirsten," he argued calmly as his dark eyes held her wrathful glare.

"I can't afford to believe anything you say." She attempted to walk past him, down the short path leading to the cabin, but his fingers took hold of the crook in her arm.

"I just want to be with you for a while."

"Of course you do—so that you can pump me for information or snoop around my cabin and then go chase after clues. Look, Dane, I know that you went to *The Herald* and I know that you were trying to dig up some more information against me because of that article on Ginevra."

He seemed unperturbed as she challenged him. His square jaw remained rigid, but his eyes had softened as he gazed down at her. "I'm just trying to understand you."

She swallowed against the bitter taste of deception. "You're just trying to gather as much information against me as you can in order to prove that I'm a paranoid woman hell-bent to squeeze every last dime out of KPSC."

"I don't think that at all." His hazel eyes had clouded and his thick, dark brows drew together in an uncompromising scowl. She raised a doubtful eyebrow in disdain. "You're the most infuriating woman I've ever met," he muttered as he let go of her arm and pushed his hands into the pockets of his jeans.

"Maybe it's just the company I keep," she retorted. "If you'll excuse me—"

"I'd like to," he admitted. "Oh, lady, I wish I could just excuse you and leave you alone."

Her voice stumbled over the anger in her words. "Well, now's your big chance," she whispered.

"You're asking me to leave?" He stared at her intently, watching every trace of emotion evidenced in her confused green eyes.

Kirsten nodded mutely, the words never passing her lips. More than anything in the world she wanted Dane to stay with her and hold her in the security of his protective arms. But she couldn't.

"Why?" he asked.

"Because you scare me, damn it." Her voice quavered as she met his relentless gaze. "You scare the hell out of me, and I don't know how to deal with it."

"Because of who I am?"

She shook her head, fighting to keep the unwanted tears from pooling in her eyes. "Maybe," she murmured in a voice barely audible over the sound of the surf crashing against the sand. "I can't seem to forget that your mission in life is to try to prove that I'm nothing more than a chisling employee bearing a grudge."

"Don't think of me as the attorney for the defense," he suggested.

"Oh, Dane." The pain in her eyes overshadowed

her anger and managed to disguise her love. "Don't patronize me. I'm an intelligent woman and I know why you're here, why you're interested."

"You don't know a damned thing," he replied as he extracted his hands from the safety of his pockets to reach up and capture her shoulders. Warm fingertips caressed her skin and drew her body close to his. Lips, cooled by the cold sea air, touched hers tentatively.

She closed her eyes to reality. The response within her was immediate. A warm, uncoiling desire flooded her senses. The muscles that had previously ached were soothed as his lips pressed against hers. The scent of the sea mingled with the earthy male odor uniquely his. She sighed in despair when his lips drew away from hers.

"I've thought of nothing but you for the past two weeks," he admitted raggedly when he lifted his head from hers.

"I'll bet," she said.

"Shhh. It's not like that." His hazel eyes, filled with questions and pain, searched her face. "I wanted to be with you, not as opponents in the courtroom, but as a man to a woman."

"It's not that easy—"

"It's as easy as you make it," he whispered against her hair, and he held her gently to him. "I've wanted you, Kirsten, ached for you these past couple of weeks."

"But I haven't heard a word from you—you didn't call."

"Because that's the way I thought you wanted it." His arms tightened around her body and his hands pressed possessively against her back. "I knew that I couldn't . . . touch you over the phone . . . that I wouldn't be able to see into your eyes." His lips pressed soft kisses into her damp hair. "And I promised myself that I would look into those eyes again, not from across the courtroom, but here, alone, by the sea."

She felt her reservations melting, knew that her determination was crumbling with the power of his words. "It's not that I don't want to trust you," she admitted. "It's that I can't!"

He held her flushed face between his hands and forced her eyes to reach into the depths of his. "Let yourself go for just a little while."

"I did before . . . you used me."

The wind swirled restlessly around them, cooling the air as night began its imminent descent. Dane closed his eyes and held her as if he were afraid she might disappear. "I've done a lot of things I'm not proud of in my life, but you've got to believe that I've never abused you."

"Strong words—"

"The truth."

"What do you want from me?" she asked, giving in to the raw female urges of her body.

He chuckled deep in his throat. "Nothing sinister, I assure you. I'd just like to take you to dinner."

She shook her head. "I don't think so. What if someone saw us? Not only would Lloyd quit the case, he'd probably skin me alive."

"He'll never know."

She smiled in spite of herself. "Already you're suggesting that I lie to my attorney."

"This has nothing to do with the lawsuit, remember?"

"Hmph." She eyed him suspiciously. "What if someone from the press saw us together . . . maybe even managed to get a couple of pictures?"

"Who'd recognize us?"

"Let's start with Laura Snyder of *The Herald*." Kirsten pulled out of his embrace and started walking toward the house. "You're not exactly unknown," she pointed out when Dane caught up with her. "And for several years I was a reporter for local television. I'd say we should consider ourselves a highly visible twosome. Neither one of us can afford to be seen with the other." She kicked off her running shoes and unlocked the door before holding it open and silently inviting him inside.

"What are you suggesting—a clandestine rendez-vous?" he asked with an inquisitive arch of one dark brow and a lazy half-smile.

"Isn't that what this is?"

He shrugged. "I offered to buy you dinner—"

"How about a raincheck—" she suggested, and then, realizing that it would never happen, Kirsten sobered. "Let's not think about that." She closed the door behind him. "Just give me a minute to change and I'll scrounge something up in the kitchen."

She left him to his own devices and took a quick, scalding shower before stepping into a clean pair of jeans and an emerald green blouse. Her hair was still damp and she was rolling one of the sleeves of the blouse up when she stepped into the living room.

Dane was crouched before the fireplace and poking at the smoldering logs with a piece of kindling. His jeans pulled tightly across his buttocks and strained against the muscles in his thighs. He had taken off his sweater, and through the thin fabric of a cotton shirt the muscles of his shoulders rippled as he worked.

He slid an appreciative eye in her direction. "You certainly don't dawdle," he said approvingly.

"Can't—not in my profession . . . or at least what used to be my profession."

The fire ignited, casting golden shadows into the room, and Dane stood, his eyes still appraising her as he dusted his hands on his jeans. "Are you giving up reporting?"

"Not exactly." The conversation was becoming too personal, wandering on forbidden territory, and Kirsten attempted to sidestep the issue.

Dane frowned thoughtfully. "You're a good reporter, Kirsten, you shouldn't give it up."

"That's a strange compliment considering the source."

Dane's scowl gave way to a slow-spreading smile that displayed the flash of nearly perfect white teeth. "I've seen several news clips—you knew your stuff." He cocked his head pensively. "A lady with a lot of class, savvy, intelligence and sexy enough to keep the audience interested." He chuckled at her stunned expression.

"That's what you think? Honestly? Or are you just trying to seduce me?"

"Perhaps a little of both," he admitted before turning his gaze from her face to look out the window at the dark sea. "By the way, it's not an opinion that I've spread around the office."

"I'll bet not." She warned herself that he might be disguising his true feelings; he was a master at ingratiating himself to a witness. But the honesty in his clear eyes made it difficult to doubt him. "I'd better start dinner," she said in an effort to change the course of the conversation.

He followed her into the kitchen, pulled out a chair, turned it around and straddled the seat while propping his arms and chin on the back. "Can I help?" he asked lazily.

She shook her head. "I think I'll do better on my own," she laughed, her eyes sparkling.

Content to watch her sprinkle lemon pepper on the steaks, he didn't argue. Kirsten was efficient. After lighting the propane grill outside, she set the steaks over the coals and finished slicing red onions for the salad.

In a few minutes the meal was prepared and they were seated at the small table in the kitchen.

"Let me do the honors," Dane suggested as Kirsten reached into a seldom used cupboard and extracted an unopened bottle of Bordeaux she had been saving. He took the bottle, opened it and poured the wine while she lit the candles.

"Nice touch," he said, holding a chair for her.

"What? Oh, the candles? I thought they were appropriate for a . . . 'clandestine rendezvous.' "

They managed to make small talk during the course of the meal, and the subject of the trial was carefully avoided. Kirsten learned a lot about Dane and found herself laughing at some of his more bizarre court cases.

"Do you like living in the city?" she asked, cutting a slice of French bread and offering it to him.

"There are advantages," he replied evasively. "At one time in my life I thought owning a practice in Manhattan would be all I could ever want." His eyes grew dark.

"But you changed your mind?"

"Some things in life are more important than money or fame," he observed, pushing his chair away from the table and cradling his wineglass in both hands. "I made the mistake of not realizing what was valuable in life a few years ago, and I'll never do it again." He smiled sadly before looking into her eyes. "Come on, let's go check on my fire. . . ."

Once in the living room, she took a seat on the couch and curled her legs beneath her. He sat on the floor, content to stare into the glowing embers and drink his wine.

"Are you unhappy in New York?" she asked, wanting to know everything about him.

He shrugged and his shoulder brushed against her knee. "Not really."

"But not content?"

"Restless, I guess," he said. Setting down his glass, he turned to face her. "There are things I want in life—things I haven't found in the city." His eyes reached for hers and her breath caught in her throat as she gently touched his hair with her fingertips.

Dane closed his eyes as if in unbearable pain. His hand moved and slowly slid up the outside of her thigh, rubbing against the tight fabric of her jeans and creating a warm friction on her legs. He forced himself to swallow and open his eyes. "Being with you is very special," he whispered hoarsely.

"Because it's risky?" she challenged.

"Because you're the first woman I've met in a long while who's attracted me."

"Maybe it's because I'm the opponent," she ventured, her heart leaping wildly in her chest as his hands continued their upward assault on her body.

"Maybe it's because you're the most elegant woman I've ever met." It was a simple statement and it sounded honest. Kirsten had to look away from the intensity of his angled features. She set her wineglass on the table.

When his hands reached her arms he gently pulled

her off the couch and caught her as she tumbled against him. Kirsten laughed and her thick brown hair cascaded around her face, framing her flushed cheeks and sparkling green eyes with softly tangled curls. Dane brushed a wayward honey-colored lock off her cheek before touching his lips to hers. The kiss was gentle and persuasive, catching Kirsten off guard.

"Let me love you," he insisted, his voice rough with the emotions tearing at him and the strain of his desire.

"If only you could," she replied, desperately hoping that she could believe, just for this one magical night, that he loved her.

He let out a disgusted sigh and his jaw became rigid. "Oh, lady, if only you knew." His fingers twined in the thick strands of her hair. The fire's glow softened the dark corners of the room and the shadows in his eyes. When his lips found hers the kiss was demanding, and she sighed against the insistence of his supple tongue. Delicious warm feelings washed over her as he shifted and his tongue probed more deeply into the moist recess of her mouth.

Her heart pounded mercilessly in her chest, resounding in her eardrums. Tracing the lithe muscles beneath his shirt, Kirsten's fingers slowly caressed his back. She felt the tension in his spine and knew that he was suffering from the same primal urges that were taking charge of her body and mind.

Her skin became heated, her cheeks flushed and she returned the ardor of Dane's kiss with all the intensity of the fires of desire slowly consuming her.

"I've missed you," she whispered into the shell of his ear. "Oh, God, Dane, I've missed you."

His fingers toyed with the button on her jeans. When it slid through the hole, he tugged at the hem of her blouse, gently extricating the soft green fabric. She shivered when his hands touched the warm skin covering her abdomen and the tips of his fingers dipped seductively beneath the waistband of her jeans. Involuntarily her abdomen tightened, allowing room for him to touch her, inviting him to explore all of her.

His lips moved downward, leaving a moist path in their wake. They caressed her cheeks, brushed against her neck and rested at the exposed hollow of her throat. His tongue rimmed the delicate bones at the base of her throat, gently probing the soft hollow and making the blood in Kirsten's veins pulse heatedly through her body. Her fingers tensed over his back and stroked him savagely, displaying the frustrated longing raging within her.

The lowest button of her blouse slipped through the hole. Dane lowered his head and kissed the pliable skin covering her abdomen as he unbuttoned the next pearl in his path. The cool air touched her skin and his tongue moistened her flesh. His hands traveled upward and slowly, torturously, the blouse was removed to display the fullness of her breasts, straining upward, the taut dark nipples distended and waiting.

He shifted to look at her and his eyes traveled hungrily over her naked torso, which gleamed from the reflection of firelight on the thin sheen of perspiration covering her body. "Dear Lord, but you're incredible," he rasped and Kirsten could feel his despair cutting through the night.

When his fingers touched her breast she trembled in anticipation and moaned in contentment as his lips tugged gently on the nipple. His teeth teased her, tormenting her with a bittersweet pleasure akin to pain, and his hands slid down the smooth muscles of her back to settle beneath her jeans and ignite the womanly fires of desire smoldering within her.

"Let me stay with you tonight," he whispered, pulling her atop him and gently easing her jeans over her hips. "Let me stay and make love to you until dawn."

"It's more than I could hope for," she murmured, her passion blinding her to rational thought.

"Then promise me that there will be no regrets," he insisted, one gentle hand pressing against her back, forcing her to lay on him so that her breast filled his mouth.

"No regrets," she said, her throat dry, her heartbeat erratic. She felt the sweet pressure of his tongue and lips on her and she clung to him, reveling in the heat he inspired. While still wrapped in his embrace she helped him remove his clothes and slowly traced the swirling hairs around each of his nipples.

His hands forced her legs apart and he stroked her thighs, smoothing the lean muscles and preparing her for the rapturous moment he would claim her as his own.

"I love you, Kirsten," he promised as he slowly rotated her and forced her onto the faded carpet before the blood-red embers of the fire. The words spoken brought tears to her eyes, and when he pressed her legs apart with his knees, he felt her welcoming shudder of anticipation. "No regrets," he whispered, kissing a salty tear off her cheek and slowly entering her, bringing the union of her flesh to his in slow, powerful strokes of love that took her breath away and made her heart race.

The tempo increased and his breathing became as ragged as her own. The night became a sensual swirl of firelight and heat as their bodies melded to become one in a rush of liquid fire and shuddering surrender.

"Don't ever leave me," Kirsten cried in her moment of weakness.

"Never, dear one," he vowed as his body stiffened and the sweet pain of his weight crushed against her. "I'll always take care of you."

Chapter Eleven

$\mathcal{K}$irsten awoke early, just as the first golden rays of a beautiful July morning were streaming through the open window. A soft breeze gently rustled the draperies and scented the bedroom with the tangy odor of the sea. Kirsten smiled to herself and stretched while remembering the passion-filled hours of the night before.

Dane was still asleep. One dark arm was stretched possessively over Kirsten's abdomen while the other dangled over the edge of the bed. His sharp features had tempered and the lines near the corners of his eyes had softened. The night's growth of his beard shadowed his chin, but his face was unworried in slumber. Tenderly, Kirsten brushed a wayward lock of sable-brown hair out of his eyes.

He groaned and turned his head into the pillow before shifting his weight and opening one wary eye against the bright sunlight invading the room. As

Dane's eyes focused and he recognized Kirsten's intriguing green gaze, a drowsy half smile tugged at the corners of his mouth.

"Good morning," he mumbled as he pushed his fingers through his hair. The arm over her abdomen tightened and he propped himself with his free hand. His smile broadened seductively as he gazed into the vibrant depths of her green eyes. "This could become a habit," he growled affectionately.

She laughed lightly and shook her head. "Unlikely, I'm afraid."

"You wouldn't want every morning to be like this one?" His thick brows rose dubiously as his eyes slid downward over the lavender sheet draped seductively over the curves of her body. His gaze lingered for a moment at the swell of her breasts, and one strong finger toyed with the smooth fabric stretched provocatively over her nipples.

"Logistics wouldn't allow it, counselor."

"You could move to New York—"

"Sure I could." She laughed. "And do what?"

"Newscasting—"

"Me and every other reporter in the country." She shook her head, but her eyes sparkled frivolously. "I'll take my chances here, thank you." The teasing smile with its wayward dimple sobered slightly as she stared into the incredible depths of his knowing eyes. Her voice became a whisper. "That is, if you leave me any chances."

The strong arm around her tightened and he softly kissed the thoughtful pout on her lips before brushing her hair away from her worried face. "I thought we weren't going to talk about the lawsuit—wasn't that part of the bargain? Your ground rules," he reminded her.

"I remember," she said, and avoided the contemplative look in his eyes by staring out the window to the sea. "You're so right, counselor," she agreed, forcing her infectious smile once again to her lips. Kirsten was determined to forget the lawsuit—if only for a little while. When she brought her attention back to his face, she smiled wickedly and threw back the covers, exposing his nude form. "What do you say about a run on the beach?"

He didn't seem to notice that he was lying uncovered. "Didn't you already do that?"

"That was yesterday."

He laughed at her spirit. "How about a walk? Humor me, I'm older than you."

Her eyes slid seductively down his body. "And not exactly out of shape." She touched the lean muscles of his thighs and calves with her fingernail and watched him stiffen. "It's my guess that you jog every day in Central Park."

"That's the trouble with you reporters, always taking the facts and twisting them into a story."

"And lawyers are different, I suppose."

His eyebrows rose and his grin broadened. "You don't give up, do you?"

"Part of my on-the-job training."

His eyes narrowed to gleam devilishly as he rubbed his chin with his thumb. "Someone should teach you a lesson, you know."

"And let me just take a guess who'll volunteer for the job," she responded throatily, gazing at him through the thick sweep of gentle brown lashes.

"No job, Kirsten. A pleasure." In a lithe movement he hoisted his body upward and pinned her to the bed before she had the chance to argue or escape. His naked muscles moved suggestively over hers and the warm invitation in her eyes heated his blood. "A pleasure I could spend the rest of my life extracting from you."

"Promises, promises . . ." she teased.

The weight of his body combined with the feel of his supple muscles rippling sensually against hers, made her head reel. She stared into the erotic depths of his hazel eyes and her breathing became shallow and fast. When his lips touched hers she wrapped her arms around him and returned the passion of his kiss fervently.

Sunlight gave his skin a golden glow and colored his eyes an intriguing shade of gilt-edged green. His hands slid familiarly over her breasts and hips, molding her skin, kneading her firm flesh and inspiring warm liquid sensations to swirl in a torturous lover's spiral deep within her.

Her breath was caught in her throat and her teeth sank into her lips as he kissed her breasts, leaving the dark nipples moist and aching for more of his sensual touch. His hand massaged each pliant mound as his tongue traveled from one delicious nipple to the next. Her back arched off the bed in readiness and he gently kissed her abdomen; her heart thundered in her chest with the agony of her need. Her fingers twined in the thick strands of his coarse hair when his tongue lapped leisurely upward, past her navel, between her breasts, against her collarbones to lick the sensitive skin near her ear.

"You're delightful," he murmured against her ear, "but addictive." Her skin tingled. "I don't think I can ever get enough of you."

"I hope not," she said raggedly.

When his lips returned to hers his fingers caught in her hair and he kissed her with a consuming passion that made her blood flow in molten rivulets throughout her body. She felt his knees move to position himself between her legs and she gasped when he entered her, savoring the sweet pleasure that his swift, sure strokes inspired.

She closed her eyes and emitted a sigh of pleasure as the heat pulsed through her body. His breathing was erratic and rapid when she felt the first bursting spasm of love overtake her. Reality blurred as the consuming tides of surrender rushed through her. Her throat was dry and hoarse when she called his name before letting her teeth sink into the hard muscles of his shoulder. The taste of his perspiration lingered on her lips as he moaned against her ear and the weight of his body crushed her against the sheets.

Dane and Kirsten walked side by side in the wet sand. The lonely cry of sea gulls could be heard over the tireless roar of the surf. Kirsten's hands were plunged deep into the pockets of her light jacket and Dane's arm was draped protectively over her shoulders. She felt oddly at peace with the world and knew that the unreal sensation could never last.

"This is insane, you know," Kirsten ventured. The walk beside the sea had been sobering and the laughter and gaiety of her morning with Dane had already faded into a quiet, secret memory. They had breakfasted on sweet melon, muffins and hot coffee laced with brandy. Now, as she thought about the fated trial separating them, the morning happiness they had shared seemed a lifetime ago.

Kirsten slid a sidelong glance at Dane. A soft breeze blew his dark hair away from his face, displaying all too vividly the lines of concern creasing his forehead. His thoughts must have taken him unhappily back to reality, as had hers.

"We can't very well continue an affair without someone finding out about it," she thought aloud, her soft green gaze searching the horizon as if for an answer to her unwanted love for this man.

"Does that worry you?" he asked.

"Yes."

"Are you ashamed?" His voice was low, his hazel eyes troubled.

"Of course not—it's just the trial." She shook her head. "That damned trial."

"You could drop the case," he suggested with a shrug of his broad shoulders.

Her head snapped upward and her angry eyes drilled into his. "Is that what you want?"

"What I want isn't the question."

"This case is important to me, Dane, and I'm not about to give up on it now." Her voice was soft, but filled with resolve. "And if you think that you can come down here, jump into my bed and then talk me out of suing KPSC, you've got another think coming!"

"I wouldn't even want to try," he said. "It's just that the lawsuit isn't making much sense—at least not to me."

"Why not?" Her bright green eyes met his defensively.

"I can't buy the age-discrimination thing. I told you that before."

Her temper got the better of her and she stopped dead in her tracks to face him bitterly. "Then why don't you go work for KPSC? I'm sure you'd catch on very quickly."

"I talked to Aaron Becker."

"And you didn't get any straight answers," she surmised.

"I can't say for certain—"

"Of course you can't. You're an attorney—defending him and that station of his."

Dane smiled grimly. "I'll admit that he did seem to avoid some of the more sensitive issues."

"More sensitive issues? What's that supposed to mean? You're hedging, Dane, just like Aaron Becker," she charged, placing her hands resolutely on her hips.

"Maybe I am," he admitted. "It seems I've got myself caught in the middle—"

"Then let's not talk about it. I wouldn't want you to jeopardize the case, counselor," she bit out angrily. Pulling free from the protection of his arm, Kirsten started walking back to the cabin. Her small fists clenched at her sides and she was muttering under her breath. What did she expect from Dane? That he would believe anything she would say and take it as gospel? Attorneys didn't work that way, she reminded herself bitterly.

She was on the weathered stairs before she turned to see if Dane was following her. He wasn't. Standing where she had left him, Dane stared out to sea. There was something about his lone form staunchly watching the restless tide that disturbed Kirsten and twisted her heart. "Why you?" she whispered as she cast one final searching look at him. "Why not Lloyd Grady or anyone else? Why did I have to fall in love with you?" Finding no answers to her question, Kirsten started up the stairs.

Dane had considered the fact that he might be defending the wrong side of the issue as far as the

McQueen case was concerned. His determination was based on sound judgment and had little to do with the fact that he was incredibly attracted to the plaintiff. Or so he told himself as he watched the dark silhouette of a ship sliding silently across the distant horizon.

Harmon Smith's attitude along with the opinions voiced by Fletcher Ross and Aaron Becker reinforced Dane's fears that Kirsten was being abused and sacrificed for the sake of KPSC's reputation. The idea that Kirsten was being set up as a scapegoat sickened Dane and made his blood boil in anger and frustration. Despite his earlier promise to Harmon Smith, Dane knew he couldn't be a part of the character assassination of Kirsten McQueen.

The distant ship became a small speck on the blue expanse of sky and sea. Staring at the calm waters of the Pacific, Dane told himself that he shouldn't care what happened to Kirsten, that he shouldn't pursue the issue and that his entire career was on the line. Pushing his palms into the back pockets of his jeans, he kicked at a broken sand dollar and realized that he really didn't give a damn about his career or any hastily made promises to a man the likes of Smith.

If Smith were lying, as Dane suspected, Dane's career would suffer anyway and Dane had promised himself that he would never make the same naive error he had about the Stone Motor Company. He had come to Kirsten's cabin near Cape Lookout searching for the truth, and come hell or high water, he was determined to find it.

But he needed Kirsten's help. He had to get information from Kirsten, not trap her as he had originally planned, but discover the truth. He started to walk up the beach back to the cabin and smiled as he followed Kirsten's deeply etched footprints.

Lloyd Grady would refuse to help him—that much was certain. The Portland attorney had insisted that Dane stay away from his client until the case had been tried. Dane didn't blame Lloyd—it was the same advice he would give his client, should the situation be reversed.

However, he had ignored Lloyd's warning and come to this lonely stretch of sand and sea to look for Kirsten. He had paid little attention to the fact that he might well be risking the entire suit by seeing Kirsten again, and had decided to let the cards fall where they may. He had been determined to see Kirsten and find out for himself what it was about Ginevra, Oregon, that bothered Harmon Smith and made him sweat.

Casting a final, rueful look at the sea, Dane strode across the final stretch of powdery sand. He climbed the staircase angling upward along the cliff and remembered the first time he had seen Kirsten on the newsclip in Harmon Smith's office. From the minute he had stared at her incredible green eyes he had known that she wasn't the liar Harmon Smith had insisted she was.

Kirsten was sipping coffee and studying several neatly typed pages on her lap. Her reading glasses were perched on the end of her nose and she didn't look up when she heard Dane enter the cabin.

"Research?" he asked cautiously, still standing near the door. Kirsten wondered if he intended to escape.

"Um-hum. An article I plan to do on Ecola State Park—it's just a few miles north of here. Interesting place; good view of the ocean and lots of wildlife.

Sea-lion and bird rookeries are located on off-shore rocks, and deer are supposed to roam through the park. Since this is for a nature magazine, it should be an inspiring article."

"Kirsten—"

She lifted her eyes to meet his disarming gaze. "What is it, Dane?" she asked, removing her glasses and her hostile manner.

"I think we should talk." He leaned against the door and observed her. Wearing little makeup and faded jeans, her hair unruly from the wind and her smile patiently frail, he decided she was the most beautiful woman he had ever known.

"There's nothing left to say." She sighed. "We've been over this all before, Dane." Her hands were trembling and she forced herself to take a long sip of coffee before she could trust herself to speak again. "Maybe you should leave now," she suggested.

"If that's what you really want." His voice was hoarse.

"It's a problem, isn't it? What I want, I mean. I'm not really sure myself anymore." She shook her head at the unfathomable thought and tears ran down her cheeks. "Me, the woman who knew just what she wanted in life and how to get it."

"But now you don't?"

Her smile was wistful and her eyes burned with unwanted tears. "Now I don't," she agreed. "And do you know why? It's because of you, damn it. You turn my head around, change my perspective, alter my objectivity. I know I shouldn't trust you, and I want to more desperately than I've wanted anything in my life." She sighed and her gaze became self-mocking. "The worst part of it is that I'm acting like a teen-ager."

She shook her head as if disgusted with herself. "I'm a thirty-five-year-old woman. In a few more months I'll be thirty-six. I always thought I had it together. Even through the pain of the divorce I knew I would find a way to survive. And I did. Somehow I managed to pull through." Her green eyes held his concerned gaze. "But with you it's different," she whispered, her voice catching. "I can't see any way of resolving this relationship, and sometimes I just want to sit down and cry my eyes out."

"But you don't let yourself," he guessed.

"I try not to. I'm not a child, Dane, and I don't want to act or feel like one."

"Is that what I do to you?"

"That and a whole lot more," she conceded wearily. "Would you like some coffee?"

He shook his head. "I can get it later." He noticed the tears in her eyes and her trembling fingers as she balanced the earthenware mug. "I've never meant to hurt you," he said, damning himself for the pain she was bearing.

"I know."

"I think I'm falling in love with you—"

"Don't!" She fought against the tears and held her hand out to forestall any vain promises. "Let's not complicate this with love," she whispered.

"I'm not a man to say things I don't mean." He leaned forward on his knees and clasped his hands in front of him. His features, angled and hard, were strained with the intent of his words. "I love you, Kirsten. You'll have to live with that whether you like it or not."

She shook her head, her honey-brown hair shimmering in the soft light with her denial. "I can't afford to love you, Dane, and I'd think you'd have the good sense to realize that the same is true for you." Tears glistened in her eyes and she apologetically brushed them away.

"Look at me," she demanded. "I'm a mess." His eyes, shadowed with an angry pain, held her gaze. "I'm a professional woman; I've seen things in my line of work that would make most men ill. And I could handle it! But here I am, crying like a baby, all because of my feelings for you."

"Because of the lawsuit."

"Because you're the attorney for the defense."

"Would it change things between us if I dropped the case?"

She was instantly wary and her eyes narrowed suspiciously. "Just like that?" she asked, snapping her fingers. "Why, Dane?"

"Because I'm not sure I believe the men I'm working for."

"Harmon Smith?"

"For starters. I think I'll throw in Fletcher Ross and Aaron Becker for good measure. As a matter of fact, the only person who seems to be telling me anything worthwhile is Frank Boswick, an assistant to Smith. Ever heard of him?"

Kirsten shook her head thoughtfully as Dane continued. "I don't even think you've leveled with me, Kirsten."

"I've answered all your questions."

"But you've evaded some as well—especially about this Ginevra thing. Frank Boswick seems to think Ginevra's the reason you were fired from KPSC. Is that so?"

Kirsten hesitated. "I—I don't know if we should be talking about this."

"You can trust me."

"I don't know—"

Abruptly he stood up, walked over to her, took the cup from her hands and placed his hands on her shoulders. "Lady, you're stuck with me. One way or another I'm going to find out about all of this, not just because of that damned lawsuit, but because I want to help you!"

"By defending Harmon Smith and Aaron Becker!"

His fingers tightened over her shoulders and the gleam in his eye became perilous. He started to shake some sense into her and stopped. "You haven't heard a word I've said." Her green eyes studied the honesty in his gaze. "I love you," he vowed, his voice thick.

Kirsten's hard exterior cracked and the tears threatening all morning began to spill. "But you're working for Smith—"

"Blast it, woman! Let me help you. Just answer my questions honestly. We can deal with Smith later."

"I don't know," she whispered, her voice faltering, her heart twisting in agony.

His fingers gentled and he pulled her to him. Strong arms surrounded her and he kissed the top of her head tenderly. Kirsten softened against him and let her knees grow weak. She could feel Dane's strength surrounding her, hear the rhythmic beating of his heart.

"What do you want to know?" she whispered quietly.

"Everything."

Chapter Twelve

$\mathcal{L}$ et's start with Ginevra," Dane suggested, sitting on the corner of the couch and taking a long swallow of his coffee. Kirsten was huddled on the opposite end of the sofa and her chin was resting on her knees. "Why do you think everyone's so touchy about it?"

Kirsten shook her head and her lips compressed into a thoughtful pout. "Good question, counselor. I don't really know much about Ginevra other than it's the proposed site for the next nuclear power plant in Oregon. There's lots of controversy, largely because of the failure of the Washington Public Power Supply System and all the national attention given to the pros and cons of nuclear power."

"Has the site been approved?"

"All the preliminary paperwork has been done, but there hasn't been an official announcement. At least not yet."

In the ensuing silence Dane finished his coffee, set the cup aside and tossed Kirsten's story over in his mind. "Aaron Becker didn't want you to cover the story?"

"He didn't want me near it."

"Surely the station had to give it some attention."

"Oh, they did. KPSC did a series of two-minute reports on Ginevra one week." Dane's jaw tensed as if he had discovered an inconsistency in her story. Kirsten felt a moment of remorse. Maybe, after all, he was just looking for a way to trap her in the courtroom. "Anyway, all the reports ended up to be were very shallow interviews of local people. You know, 'How do you, Mrs. Ginevra Homemaker, feel about construction of the site? Couldn't this be the economic boom the town needs? Wouldn't it give all of the unemployed citizens a chance to get back to work?'"

"You think that the reports were slanted, to give the public a positive view of Ginevra as the potential site."

"I don't know. It just seemed strange to me that with all the controversy over nuclear power, nothing negative was ever cast from KPSC, at least as far as I know."

"So you wanted to do an in-depth study on Ginevra, report the negative aspects as well as the positive."

"Right." Kirsten smiled bitterly and her green eyes widened with indignation as she remembered the tense moment when she had asked for the assignment and Aaron Becker had at first paled and then had laughed outright. "Forget it, sweetheart," Becker had commanded, still chuckling in nervous amusement. "You're better off covering that bake-off in St. Johns.

Stick to things you understand." Kirsten's blood had boiled and she had left Aaron Becker's office determined to report on something more pressing than a local cooking contest.

"And Becker refused to let you report on it."

"That's putting it mildly." Kirsten's legs were crossed and her left foot bounced in agitation.

"But there were other stories you wanted to cover and were denied—other than Ginevra, that is."

"Yes." Kirsten sighed wearily. "After I started asking about Ginevra, everything else I wanted to do was given to someone else."

"Someone younger?"

"Most of the time."

"But usually male," Dane guessed, and he noticed the spark of anger lighting Kirsten's eyes.

"This is not a sex-discrimination suit," she reminded him. "The reason that most of the stories were given to men is that most of the reporters for KPSC are men."

"So that brings us to the age-discrimination suit," Dane remarked, watching Kirsten's reaction. She held her head high, her chin tilted regally.

"I guess it does."

He settled back in the corner of the couch and studied her with undisguised interest. "Tell me about it."

Kirsten hesitated only slightly. "Nothing so out of the ordinary, I guess. I'd been getting in some hot water with Aaron about the other stories I wanted to cover. I wanted to do something a little meatier than covering the selection of the Rose Festival Court or the remodeling of the Grand Theatre."

"Or the bake-off in St. Johns?"

Kirsten was forced to laugh. "Uh-huh. Until I started making noise about different stories, Aaron seemed satisfied with my work, but once I started asking for more interesting assignments, Aaron became sullen and started nitpicking everything I did."

"So what does this have to do with age discrimination?" Dane inquired.

Kirsten took in a long, steadying breath. Until this point everything she had told Dane was fact. Now she was going into nebulous territory: part fact, part conjecture on her part. "I was sure that Aaron was trying to phase me out of my job."

"How?" Dane's hazel eyes sharpened; he sensed her unease.

Kirsten stared into the bottom of her empty cup. "I'd seen it happen before, when a woman reporter became a little too old or outspoken to suit Aaron's tastes."

"So sexual discrimination was involved."

"To some extent, yes," Kirsten admitted. "Aaron preferred younger women in front of the camera, women who looked as good on film as they did in his bed."

"Do you know what you're suggesting?" Dane asked, his voice low and his brooding eyes narrowing suspiciously.

"I know exactly what I'm saying," she assured him, her finely sculpted jaw elevating slightly.

Dane studied her dubiously and Kirsten knew that he was reassessing her. She knew she was beginning to sound like some of the gossiping women she detested, but she felt that Dane had to understand her position. If she were ever going to make him believe her, Kirsten had to tell him everything she knew. If he used it against her later—well, she would have to deal with his betrayal of confidence then.

"He expected you to sleep with him?" Dane's eyes darkened perilously.

The corners of Kirsten's mouth quirked. "It would have helped me with my job." The look of fire in Dane's hazel eyes made Kirsten's blood run cold. "Don't get me wrong. I didn't mean to imply that every woman who worked at KPSC slept with Aaron Becker. That's not the case."

"I wouldn't think so," he said, his temper barely restrained. Why did the thought of any man touching Kirsten make his jaw tighten and his fists clench? Dane wasn't a savage man by nature, but there was something about Kirsten that made him want to protect her from anything and anyone to the point of ruthlessness. "What about you?"

"I'd like to tell you that it's none of your business, counselor, and you can bet that if you ask me these questions on the witness stand, I will." The conversation was becoming more dangerous by the minute.

"But it is my business," he reminded her angrily.

Her clear green eyes didn't flinch under his wrathful stare. "I haven't slept with a man since my divorce—until you. I'm not comfortable with the idea of casual sex."

"I know that. I just find it hard to believe that you got away unscathed—if Aaron Becker is the lech you say he is."

"Then you should know that I would never allow Aaron Becker, or any other man I work with, to touch me. Aaron was my boss. We had a professional relationship, nothing more."

"Not from any lack of want on his part, I'll wager,"

Dane decided as he rubbed his shoulders and tried to dissolve the tension from the muscles at the base of his neck.

"He made a couple of passes at me, if that's what you mean. During my separation and divorce from Kent."

Dane's hand stopped massaging his neck and his eyes grew deadly dark. "But you managed to deter him?" Dane sounded skeptical and his back teeth crushed together at the vivid scene in his mind.

"I've had a lot of practice," she admitted, taking her eyes away from him for a moment and setting her empty cup on the table. "Aaron got the message that I wasn't interested, and after a while he left me alone—that is until I turned thirty-five and started asking questions about Ginevra."

"Then he fired you." Dane's voice was flat, hiding the rage and indignation burning in his chest.

"That's about the size of it."

When Dane considered the ego of Aaron Becker, his jaw tightened and his back became rigid with tension. Dane remembered the interview with Becker where the man had insinuated that Kirsten had thrown herself at him wanting sexual favors.

"So what are you going to do now?" he asked, forcing his voice to remain even.

"Other than the lawsuit?" Kirsten asked. Dane nodded mutely, his eyes never leaving her face. "I'm looking for another job."

"In Portland?"

"Are you kidding? With all the publicity of the lawsuit, I don't have a prayer of getting hired in Portland. Or Seattle either." She looked at the ceiling. "I've sent résumés to several stations in San Francisco and L.A., but so far I haven't had any response. It's getting to be a problem though," she admitted thinking of her dwindling savings account. "Man does not live on free-lance alone, you know."

"But you won't consider New York."

She shook her head, but smiled fondly at him. "I think I'm better off here—away from you." She couldn't lie to him, as much as she would have liked to. What could be more pleasant than living near Dane, being with him?

"Are you serious?" he asked.

"Think about it, Dane. We've been kidding ourselves. How long can we continue to see each other?"

"As long as we like."

She closed her eyes and her heart twisted painfully. "We can't forget about the lawsuit. It's always there. We can't even be seen in public together."

"Look, Kirsten, there's no reason to keep rehashing this," he stated as he stood and stretched his weary muscles. "You're right. The lawsuit is a problem and it can't be resolved—not here, not today. But let's try to push it aside for just a little while, until we can sort everything out." He leaned over and gently pulled her to her feet. His eyes probed into hers as he drew her into the powerful circle of his arms. With a tenderness that warmed the deepest part of her, Dane kissed her forehead. "You worry too much," he whispered.

"Maybe because my entire future is on the line."

"Come on, let's go to dinner—"

"But we can't be seen together," Kirsten protested softly, her lips touching his shirt.

"We won't," he assured her with a devilish twinkle in his eye.

She tried to extricate herself from the comforting manacle of his arms and eyed him with dubious interest. "Just what have you got in mind, counselor?"

"Something different. Hurry up." Without any further explanation the powerful arms released her and Dane reached for her jacket hanging on the hall coat-tree and tossed it to her.

"Where are we going?" she asked with undisguised interest. "Should I change?"

"You look great." To add emphasis to his words, his eyes slid seductively down her body. "And if we don't get going soon, I might be inclined to spend the rest of the afternoon here—in bed."

"Why the mystery, counselor?" she asked as she threw her jacket over her arm and walked through the door that he held open for her.

"Keeps you interested. Admit it."

She shook her head and laughed. "Life is anything but dull when you're around," she conceded. "I just hope you know what you're doing."

"Always." He opened the door of the rental car, and when she slid into the seat he shut it again. She watched him walk around the front of the car and take the driver's seat. With a roar the engine sparked to life and Dane put the car in gear. "There's something very macho about spiriting a beautiful woman to an unknown destination, don't you think?"

Her only response was a ripple of carefree laughter.

Depoe Bay was crawling with tourists who had come to the unique coastal town. The business district of the small, bustling city was perched on the cliffs overlooking the rockbound bay that slashed inland from the broad expanse of Pacific Ocean.

"You're out of your mind," Kirsten accused him when she understood what Dane was planning.

"And you're paranoid." He parked the car and opened the door. "Do you really think any of these people"—he motioned to the crowd of brightly dressed tourists leisurely walking on the sidewalk along Highway 101—"would recognize you?"

"I'm not about to take the chance!"

Just then the spray from the Spouting Horn, a gap in the rocks through which the tide raced upward in a geyserlike spray near the sidewalk, plumed into the air. Everyone on the street stopped to view the spectacle.

"I think you're safe," Dane commented dryly as he viewed the townspeople and tourists with interest.

He slammed the car door shut and disappeared into a local fresh seafood stand. He was back within minutes carrying a white sack filled with delicacies. After placing the bag in the backseat, he slid into the driver's seat once again and drove to a less public parking lot.

When the car stopped, Kirsten turned to face him. "You rented a boat, didn't you?"

His lazy smile gave him away.

"Do you know how to operate one?" she asked.

"Don't you?"

"Of course, but—"

"Then let's go."

He opened the car door, but she placed a staying hand on his arm. "Dane . . . why?"

His eyes sobered. "I wanted to be alone with you, Kirsten, but I don't like the idea of hiding. I thought we could spend a little time enjoying ourselves instead of always arguing and brooding about the lawsuit." His fingers touched the elegant line of her jaw. "Come on." Her pulse raced at the tender gesture and she slid out of the car.

The boat was moored in the bay. To get to the gleaming white vessel Kirsten and Dane had to walk down a bleached wooden staircase that led from the small town poised on the top of the cliff to the dark waters of the bay. The stairs were located near the bridge spanning Depoe Bay and as Kirsten walked toward the moorage she noticed barnacles clinging to the pilings supporting the bridge.

The boat was small but seaworthy, and Dane maneuvered the tiny craft through the fishing vessels and pleasure boats that clogged the small body of water. Once under the bridge and out of the crowded waters of the bay, Dane headed north.

"I thought you didn't know how to handle a boat," Kirsten accused him, her voice barely heard over the roar of the engine.

"I didn't say that. I just wanted to be sure that you had your sea legs on you."

"But—I thought—I mean, you live in the city, for God's sake."

"We have an ocean on that side of the continent, too, you know," he stated with a mocking smile and wicked gleam in his eyes. After twenty minutes he cut the engine and let the boat drift on the sea. "There are a lot of things you don't know about me."

"Such as?"

"Such as the fact that I grew up in a fishing village on Cape Cod."

Kirsten withdrew the food from the white sack and handed Dane a plastic carton filled with Dungeness crabmeat and tangy cocktail sauce. They ate without breaking the silence. The sea was calm and the small craft rocked gently on the water. The afternoon would have been hot except for the slight breeze moving gently over the water. To the west, dark clouds were drifting toward the shore and threatened to destroy the late afternoon sun. Kirsten stared at the rugged Oregon coastline in the distance. The jagged cliffs and sandy beaches appeared smoky-blue through the slight haze that had begun to settle on the sea.

"You're right," she said after a thoughtful silence.

"About what?" Dane's smile was engaging. It touched the darkest corners of her soul.

"I don't know much about you." Taking a drink of the cool white wine Dane had purchased, Kirsten leaned back and squinted against the ever-lowering sun. "On the other hand, you know everything about me, don't you?"

He finished his food and wiped his hands together. The wind caught in his hair and ruffled the coffee-colored strands. "I've been briefed, if that's what you mean."

"And you've read employee records, my original résumé and any other pertinent piece of information Aaron Becker and Fletcher Ross gave you. Besides which, I'll bet you did some digging on your own."

"A little," he conceded begrudgingly. And then, as if to change the difficult subject, his eyes scanned the darkening horizon. "We'd better head in; looks like we're in for a summer storm."

He had unbuttoned his shirt in an effort to stay cool, and Kirsten watched the supple movement of his muscles as he restarted the engine and headed the small boat inland. "You've got me at a disadvantage," she persisted, loud enough to be heard over the rapidly pulsing engine.

"I doubt that, Kirsten," he muttered, his eyes clouding. "I'd like to believe it, but I don't. Not for a minute."

She eyed him lazily and smiled to herself as she

watched him guide the gently rocking craft back to its moorage in Depoe Bay. He's a handsome man, she decided, watching the jut of his square jaw and the narrowed eyes as he studied the water. His dark hair had only a few traces of gray and his lean physique was trim and well-muscled. He looked at home behind the wheel of the boat, with the wind in his face and his shirttails fluttering behind him. It was hard to imagine that he was a famous New York attorney whose job it was to discredit her. Not only was he handsome, he was shrewd as well. Shrewd enough to know exactly how to read a woman.

Dane noticed the furrow of Kirsten's brow. "What are you thinking about?" he called over his shoulder.

"Nothing," she replied, lifting her shoulders.

"You're a lousy liar, Kirsten McQueen."

"Am I? Good."

He looked at her quizzically.

"Then you'll know that I'm telling the truth when we meet in the courtroom."

His lips thinned and he turned away from her to stare back at the prow of the boat knifing through the water and study the passage back to the bay.

The drive back to the cabin had been accomplished in silence. Dane hadn't responded to her barb about the courtroom and Kirsten didn't blame him. But how could he expect her to ignore the fact that the lawsuit existed? As each day drew to a close, the impending courtroom battle loomed nearer.

Dane had gone for a solitary soul-searching walk on the beach, leaving Kirsten to stay at the cabin. She told herself that it was time to analyze her relationship with Dane. She had to clear her mind and set her roiling emotions in some sort of order. How long could they continue to ignore the fact that they would meet in the courtroom and at that point be at each other's throat? Until September tenth?

She slammed her fist on the bureau top and gazed wearily into the mirror. How could she love a man so feverishly and still not be able to trust his motives? Her tired reflection had no answers.

The evening was hot and muggy. The dense air was filled with the promise of summer rain, which would be a welcome relief to the sticky humidity.

Kirsten showered and changed into a sundress and sandals. She waited for Dane to return, and after an hour she began to worry. What was taking him so long to return? Had he been that angry with her?

Anxiously her worried eyes scanned the beach, but the sun had set and it was rapidly growing dark. Though squinting at the silvery sand, she could see no sign of him. Desperately, her eyes searched the gathering darkness, hoping to see some trace of the man she loved so futilely.

"Damn it, counselor," she muttered as she hurried out the front door and down the path leading to the steps along the cliff face. When she got to the landing of the staircase her eyes again scanned the long stretch of white sand and noted the storm clouds rolling ominously off the sea.

With one hand on the rail to balance her she raced down the stairs and started running the minute her feet hit the sand. His footprints led south. She followed them and her concerned eyes scanned the darkness. "Where the devil are you?" she asked the rising wind.

She had run for nearly a mile when she saw Dane

retracing his steps. Relief, like a welcome rain, showered her as she stopped to catch her breath and wait for him.

When he was close enough to hear her she ran to him and fell into his open arms, saying, "I was worried sick. Where have you been?"

"Walking, thinking." His arms held her tightly against him. "I thought you were angry." Storm clouds rumbled threateningly and the wind gusted around them.

She shook her head and felt the first welcome drops of rain run down the back of her neck. "Just concerned, that's all," she whispered. As she looked up she could read the sorrow in his eyes. "I just don't know where all this will lead us," she admitted. "It worries me."

"You think I'm using you," he charged, defeat evident in his words and the tired slump of his shoulders.

"No, but I can't help but wonder what will happen once we're on opposite sides of the courtroom."

He pushed a weary hand through his hair. "Maybe it won't go that far—"

She stopped dead in her tracks. "I'm not giving up the lawsuit."

"Is it that important to you?"

"Yes." Couldn't he understand, feel her rage? Did he expect her to suffer those indignities in silence—alone?

"More important than—"

"Don't, Dane. Don't even compare what I feel for you to what I have to do. It's not fair." Her voice was trembling from the depth of her feelings and she shivered as if she were suddenly chilled. Tears threatened her eyes and her throat felt uncomfortably tight.

"It's just that I don't want to lose you," he whispered, clinging desperately to her. "I have this incredible fear that when the dust has settled and the lawsuit is over I won't see you again."

She smiled upward at him. "I thought you were the one who didn't want to worry about the future."

"Is that what I said?" She nodded and he kissed the top of her head. His warm breath caught in her hair. "I must be more of a fool than I thought."

She studied the lines of his face and noticed the agony shadowed in the depths of his eyes. Dread caught in her throat. "What's this all about, Dane?"

He shrugged but wasn't released from the weight of his burden. "A lot of things, I suppose. You, me, the lawsuit, Harmon Smith." His lips drew into a disgusted frown. "Especially Smith."

"Why would you let a man like Smith bother you?" Kirsten asked. "You act as if he owns you."

"Maybe he does," was the gruff reply.

"You can't be serious." Her comment was meant as a light attempt at humor, but the darkness in Dane's face and the tightness of his skin stretched over his cheekbones indicated that his relationship with Smith was more involved than the usual one between client and attorney.

Dane released her suddenly and began walking back toward the cabin. His strides were long and determined. "What do you mean?" Kirsten asked, nearly running to keep up with him.

"I owe Smith a favor—a big favor," Dane replied, stomping angrily toward the stairs. "And it's payoff time."

"Payoff? Dane? I don't get it—" But just as the words were out of her mouth, Kirsten began to understand. The lawsuit against her! That was the payoff. The coldbloodedness of the situation hit her like a blast of arctic air. "Wait a minute," she called, but he was already to the stairs. She had to run to catch up to him. Her sandals caught on a buried piece of driftwood and she stumbled but she managed to catch herself.

Dane was already climbing the stairs. He heard her gasp and turned to face the noise.

Kirsten's throat was dry and tears began forming in her eyes. Rain from the heavens began to fall in earnest and she could feel the cool drops run down her bare back. She caught him and clutched his arm.

"What do you mean?" she choked out. "Don't tell me that you took this case to settle an old debt!"

He looked down at her with self-condemning eyes. "Would that surprise you, Kirsten?"

"I just hoped that you took the case because you wanted to and that once you found out the truth, you would drop it and—"

"Leave you alone?" he charged, his voice loud enough to be heard over the pounding surf and the rising wind. "Is that what you wanted?" His jaw was clamped rigidly, his mouth compressed into a thin, wrathful line.

He braced himself on the railing and pushed his face nearer to hers. "Then what about the seduction, Kirsten? Was that all for a quick thrill too? Or was it part of the plan? Did you intend to take me to your bed and then just let me go as soon as the case was resolved?"

"I didn't plan it at all. It just happened. Dear God, Dane, the last thing I wanted was to fall in love with you!" Her clear green eyes were filled with the honesty and pain of her confession.

He looked up to the dark sky as if asking for divine

intervention. Warm rain slid down the collar of his shirt. "Dear God, woman," he whispered, reaching his hand down toward her. It was shaking but she took it and allowed him to help her up the stairs. Breathlessly he wrapped his arms around her and kissed the raindrops off the crook of her neck.

"I'm sorry, Kirsten," he whispered against her ear. He squeezed his eyes shut as if in physical agony. "The last thing I ever want to do is hurt you . . ." His lips claimed hers in a kiss filled with promise and pain. "I love you, Kirsten," he vowed. "More than you'll ever know."

"And I love you," she vowed, holding on to him as if for dear life. "I didn't mean to get angry . . ."

"Shhh . . . it's all right." He kissed her on the forehead and then wiped the tears from her eyes. "I think I should tell you about Julie."

"Your wife?" she asked weakly.

"That's right." His voice was raw with unnamed emotions. "Maybe then you'll understand why I have to repay Harmon Smith."

Her heart thundered erratically in her chest, and she had to swallow against the dread forming in her throat. Silently, she let Dane drape his arm over her shoulders before easing her to the ground. His lips whispered against the nape of her neck.

"Don't, Dane," she whispered, the blood within her beginning to warm. "You don't have to say anything. Just make love to me and never stop."

Ignoring the cool wind and the sultry rain, he untied the thin straps holding the lavender sundress in place. The bodice of the dress fell downward, exposing each of her rosy-tipped breasts.

"You're so lovely," he breathed, touching each nipple gently with his lips before burying his face in the folds of her skirt. "So lovely." Through the thin fabric his warm breath brushed against her legs and made her quake with the need of him.

"I didn't want to love you," he said, his hands sliding suggestively up her legs.

"Nor I you," she murmured huskily.

The raindrops began to filter from the sky in increased numbers. Her hair, dress and naked breasts were moist, and his hands slid easily against her skin.

Each breast was touched, kissed and sucked until the slowly spreading fire within her began to grow white hot. It was as if the more she had of this man, the more she wanted. Her need was all-consuming.

Her hands slowly removed his clothes and her eyes touched every inch of his lean, rippling muscles. She cradled his head in her hands and offered him her breasts. He took first one and then the other into the warm moist recess of his mouth.

Kirsten sighed into the wind and felt as if she and Dane were the only two people in the universe. His hands traced her spinal column and splayed across the small of her back, gently encouraging her body more closely to his.

The warmth within her began to ache and she strained against him, hungry for him to fill that final, primal void within her.

Dane shifted and she felt the cool moist sand beneath her back. He straddled her and stared down at her, content for the moment to study every graceful line of her body. One shaking hand caressed a breast and she shuddered in anticipation before arching her body off the ground and crying out his name.

Slowly he came to her, gently parting her legs and finding the warm moist center of her womanhood. She moaned as he found her and reached up to hold him against her.

They moved as one, each offering pleasure and comfort to the other. Kirsten felt the fire and intensity build as the tempo increased, and when the final, shattering moment came, Dane whispered her name into the cool black night.

Chapter Thirteen

By the time they entered the cabin both Kirsten and Dane were soaked to the skin. The tension in the air had dissipated and Kirsten managed to laugh at the sorry sight they made in wet, bedraggled clothes.

While Dane heated the coffee and laced it with a touch of brandy, Kirsten changed into dry clothes. When she came back into the living room, a fire was crackling merrily in the fireplace. "It's too warm for a fire," she complained with a twinkle in her green eyes.

"Never." He had been kneeling on the hearth, but stood and dusted off his hands when she entered the room. His hair was still damp, and the firelight brightened the rich sable color to a sheen of gold. "When you've lived without the convenience of a fireplace for as long as I have, you learn to appreciate the smell of burning wood and the intense heat against the back of your legs."

"But it's the end of July—"

"And less than sixty degrees, unless I miss my guess."

She offered him a towel for his hair, which he refused. Instead, he captured her wrist and pulled her against his wet body.

"Wait a minute," she protested with a merry laugh. "What do you think you're doing? I just changed."

"And you look great." He seemed to revel in her distress, and cared nothing about the fact that her crisp blouse and cords were becoming as wet as the clothes she had just thrown into the hamper.

"Dane—" she said weakly, but her words were lost in her throat when he kissed the exposed column of her neck, nibbling erotically below her ear. "You're wicked, you know," she moaned as her eyes closed.

"And you love it." His arms slowly released her and she felt oddly alone without his comforting touch. After bending to retrieve the towel, which had slipped to the floor into a fluffy blue mound, he dried his neck and hair.

"Animal," she muttered with a provocative grin.

"You wouldn't have it any other way, lady," he returned, snapping the towel against her backside.

"Oh, yes, I would," she whispered, suddenly uncomfortable. Her clear green eyes probed into the hazel depths of his seductive gaze.

"What would you change?" He handed her a mug of steaming coffee and took one for himself before bracing one shoulder against the mantel and eyeing her with undisguised interest.

"For starters . . ."

He held up his hand to cut off her response. "Oh, yes, I know. The lawsuit." Shaking his head as if bewildered at the predicament of his life, he took in a long breath. "That's something we can't change—at least not now."

"So here we are, back where we started. Every time we start this conversation we end up at a stalemate." She tapped her fingers restlessly on the ceramic mug before frowning in frustration and dropping into the corner of the couch. Tucking her shoeless feet under her, she took a long sip of the warm liquid and felt it slide soothingly down her throat.

"Maybe we should try talking about something else." The smile on his face had grown tight, his voice low.

"Such as?" Her cloudy green eyes searched his.

"The reason I took on this case in the first place. It has to do with Harmon Smith and my wife."

Kirsten took in a shuddering breath. A mounting sense of dread crawled coldly up her spine. Talking about Harmon Smith made her uneasy and she wasn't sure that she wanted to hear about Dane's wife—a woman he had loved deeply. "Look, Dane, you don't have to tell me anything you don't want to. I don't expect any wild confessions from you . . . and it's not necessary to dredge up—"

"I think it is. There are things you should know."

He stared into the black depths of his cup as he collected his thoughts. Kirsten backed into the corner of the couch, bracing herself for what was to come.

"I met Julie in college," Dane announced, his voice soft and tortured. A wistful smile curved his lips, but his eyes remained dark and expressionless. "We went together for a couple of years, lived together and finally got married when I graduated from law school."

"You loved her very much," Kirsten surmised, witnessing the pain shadowing his sharp gaze.

Dane nodded. It was a slight movement, nearly imperceptible, but it acknowledged the depth of his feelings for his deceased wife. Kirsten felt as if a knife had been thrust into her heart and cruelly twisted. "We were very happy. After a few years Sam came along." Dane took his gaze away from hers and looked out the window before quietly clearing his throat.

"I was foolish, young and thought I had the world in my pocket. My practice was flourishing upstate and I'd had a couple of offers to join an established firm in Manhattan. My biggest accomplishment was defending the Stone Motor Company and the Zircon. I suppose you read about that?"

Kirsten smiled wanly and nodded.

Dropping his head into his hand, Dane slowly massaged a throbbing temple.

Kirsten remained silent, knowing that Dane was offering her a glimpse of a part of his life he rarely exposed and preferred to keep buried.

"The Stone Motor decision was a real feather in my cap," he stated as his lips thinned menacingly. "There was lots of national attention to the case and several firms in the city wanted me to come and work for them. The offers were very attractive. Full partnerships in some of the most prestigious firms in the country." When he raised his angry, self-mocking gaze to hers, Kirsten felt herself bleed for this man who had borne so much pain. Unwanted tears burned behind her eyelids.

Kirsten studied the lines of his face. It remained emotionless, other than those two glowing, angry eyes. She sensed that Dane had practiced hiding a past that was too ugly to remember.

"I thought I was on my way—" He shook his head as if to wipe away the distasteful thought. "That's the problem with youth, you feel that you're immortal, for God's sake."

He chewed thoughtfully on his lower lip and when he spoke his voice was hoarse. "And Julie . . . she was behind me every step of the way." Kirsten's stomach knotted painfully as she watched the agony in his eyes.

"Anyway, one day, when I was working at the office, Sam got sick. It was snowing and there was ice all over the roads. Julie called, and I told her to wait, that I'd be home in a couple of hours. She didn't—I don't know why, but I suppose that maybe Sam got worse." His voice faltered for a minute. "She was always worried about him because he wasn't very healthy.

"Since I had the Bronco she had to take the Zircon. She'd driven about five miles before she hit a patch of ice. The car slid sideways and rolled down an embankment." He hesitated, took a long swallow from his cup and closed his eyes, squeezing the eyelids. "Julie and Sam were killed instantly. At least that's what I was told."

"And you blame yourself," Kirsten guessed, surrendering to the hot tears pooling in her eyes.

"I had her car—because it was safer in the bad weather."

"You couldn't have known that Sam would get sick."

His dark eyes flashed angrily. "But I could have left her with the four-wheel drive, damn it! If I hadn't been so goddamn self-serving!" His fist crashed into the warm bricks of the fireplace in frustration.

"We all make mistakes," she offered lamely.

"But usually not ones that imperil the lives of the people we love. Oh, Kirsten," he moaned prayerfully. "I was still at the office when I heard about the accident. Still at the office, for God's sake! I raced like the devil over to the hospital, but it was too late."

"There's no need to talk about this," Kirsten volunteered, hoping to find a way to ease his pain. "It's all in the past and . . . and it's gone. Nothing will change that." She got to her feet and stood next to him, tentatively offering the support of her hand on his arm. "Don't carry this guilt—"

He refused the comfort of her gesture and tossed the remains of his coffee into the fire. The air sizzled as the liquid hit the flames. "But I was the one who defended the Stone Motor Company," he pointed out. "If I hadn't worked so damned hard to prove that the Zircon was safe, Julie and Sam might still be alive."

"You don't know that. It's just conjecture."

"But a chance, damn it." She turned away from the torture showing on his face. Tears had begun to stream down her face, and her stomach was knotted by futile sympathetic thoughts for him.

Dane straightened and his hands captured her shoulders, forcing her to meet his defeated gaze. Firelight cast eerie shadows on his proud face. "There's a reason I'm telling you everything," he whispered. "I think you should know about the debt I owe Harmon Smith."

"It has something to do with the accident?" she

asked, not sure that she wanted to hear any more of his confessions.

"I—I didn't handle the deaths very well, and the guilt I felt was unbearable." Kirsten believed him. He still hadn't managed to let go of the responsibility. "I spent countless nights wondering if it would have made a difference. If I hadn't defended Stone Motors, or if I had lost the suit, would Julie and Sam have survived?" His broad shoulders slumped and the fingers gripping Kirsten's arms relaxed. "In the end I sold my practice and moved to Maine. I had a small cabin, no responsibilities and enough money to buy all the liquor I needed to drink myself into oblivion, should I feel the need."

Kirsten's heart bled for him, and all the words of consolation she wanted to say stuck in her throat. It was obvious that he had loved his family very dearly and that guilt was still gnawing painfully at him.

"I don't think I would have ever considered practicing law again if it hadn't been for Harmon Smith."

"What did Smith do?" Kirsten asked, pressing her ear to his chest and listening to the steady, rhythmic beating of his heart.

"He pulled me out of the bottle." Dane's arms tightened around Kirsten, but he avoided looking into her eyes, preferring to stare out the window at the stormy night. "Harmon Smith was an old family friend. He was close to my father and my uncle. He came to see me after my father died, probably at my uncle's behest, and made me an offer.

"Smith needed an attorney and he remembered me—probably because of the Stone Motor decision. My uncle gave him my address in Maine and one day he showed up on my doorstep. Fortunately it was one of my better days and he offered to finance an office for me in Manhattan at reasonable terms if I would agree to represent Stateside Broadcasting Corporation."

"So you accepted his proposal," Kirsten surmised, starting to understand the man she loved so hopelessly.

"I still had quite a bit of money left over from the sale of my practice in Buffalo, and that, along with the money I borrowed from Smith, was enough to start the practice. It was still a gamble, but one I couldn't afford to pass up." He let out a ragged sigh. "In other words, Harmon Smith saved my life. I know that I never would have accepted another case if Harmon hadn't helped me out."

"And that's the favor you owe him."

"Right." Dane released her and pushed his hands into the pockets of his jeans. After walking to the bay window he put a stocking foot on the sill, leaned on his knee and stared down at the turbulent black sea. "I still owe Harmon Smith over a hundred thousand dollars, and that doesn't begin to touch the fact that Harmon has handed me several important referrals and pushed a lot of business in my direction." He pushed impatient fingers through his hair. "I owe Harmon Smith, Kirsten."

"And he wants to be repaid?"

"Yes."

"I see," she whispered.

Dane turned from his position near the window and his eyes drilled into hers. "Then you have to know that Smith is determined to beat you—no matter what it takes."

Involuntarily, Kirsten's slender shoulders slumped, but she held her head upright. It was obvious that

Dane was caught between a rock and a hard spot. There was no way he could bow out of the suit and let Harmon Smith down. And Kirsten would never voluntarily drop the suit.

Kirsten had too much pride in herself and love for Dane to use their affair to her advantage. She realized that KPSC might back off if she let it be known that she had slept with the defending attorney, but she couldn't bring herself to stoop that low, not even against KPSC.

"I guess there's just no easy answer," she murmured.

"Maybe there never is." Dane didn't try to talk her out of the lawsuit again and she didn't offer. They were both trapped by their love and the hopeless circumstances that bound them.

She walked over to him and placed a comforting hand on his shoulder. "I'm tired," she whispered. "Come on, let's go to bed."

He smiled sadly and shook his head. "I'll be there in a minute," he murmured, gently kissing her forehead. She left him alone to stare out the window at the black night.

It was several hours later, after she had dropped into a fitful sleep, that she was awakened by the urgent persistence of his hands and lips on her body.

The morning dawned foggy. Kirsten slipped quietly out of bed and watched Dane as he slept. The worries of the night before seemed to have melted with sleep and his face was relaxed and unlined. She smiled sadly at him before tenderly touching the tips of her fingers to his strong jaw. He groaned and shifted on the bed.

Without disturbing him she eased off the bed, changed into her shorts and T-shirt before collecting her running shoes on the porch. Though the fog still clung to the beach, Kirsten suspected it would burn off before afternoon and she would spend another glorious day with Dane.

She didn't think about the fact that he hadn't mentioned when he intended to leave, but Kirsten hoped that he would stay through the weekend. Life without him would be very lonely, very lonely indeed.

Shrugging off any lingering doubts, she started down the small trail leading to the stairs. She was smiling by the time she reached the weathered steps. After properly stretching her legs, Kirsten started northward on her early morning run, carefully avoiding the debris that had been kicked up on the sand by last night's turbulent tide. The sea air, fresh after the storm, cooled her lungs, and she felt the exhilaration of the exercise.

It was nearly an hour later when she returned to the cabin. She was winded and covered with perspiration, but managed to race up the stairs at the thought of surprising Dane.

As she kicked off her shoes and leaned against the railing surrounding the porch to stretch her muscles, she heard signs of life from within the cabin and realized that Dane had already awakened. The shower was running and the bed was empty.

After rinsing her face and hands she changed into her robe and knocked on the bathroom door to let him know that she had returned.

The thought of joining him in the shower entered her mind, but she rejected it when she touched the door to the bathroom and noticed that it was locked. With a shrug of her shoulders she turned her attention to breakfast.

The bacon was just beginning to sizzle when she heard the shower stop. By the time Kirsten heard him enter the room, breakfast was cooked.

She didn't look up, but felt the tingle of his cool lips against her neck. "I would have joined you," she said, smiling, "but the door was locked."

"A habit," he replied.

She turned and smiled at him. "Habit?"

"Obviously you've never had children."

"Oh . . ." The sadness in his eyes when he looked at her told her he was leaving.

"They aren't particularly interested in giving you any privacy."

"I—I suppose not." She smiled despite the horrible pang of sorrow knifing through her heart. "You're going back, aren't you?"

"I have to."

"I . . . thought you might stay through the weekend," she murmured, trying not to give in to the sadness overtaking her and failing miserably.

"Business."

Her voice was unsteady when he came over to her and tilted her head upward, forcing her to gaze into his eyes. "Will it always be this way?"

"I hope not. Look, I'll be back."

"Promise?"

His smile broadened. "What do you think?"

"I wish I knew," she whispered, motioning for him to take a seat.

"Trust me," he insisted, planting a warm kiss on her lips before sliding into a chair.

And she did. With all of her heart she trusted him.

Small talk prevailed during the light meal, and it wasn't until Dane had pushed his plate aside that his eyes became serious and intent while assessing her.

"Why didn't you have kids?" he asked.

Kirsten shifted her eyes away. "Kent didn't want them. And, well, I knew that our marriage wasn't very strong."

"So you divorced him?"

"It wasn't that easy," she said, sighing. "I wanted to make it work. Even when I found out about his girlfriend . . . well, I thought we could work it out. I made an appointment with a marriage counselor. He wouldn't go."

Dane was deep in thought. "I find it hard to believe that he wouldn't have fought for you tooth and nail." His dark brows drew over his eyes in puzzling agitation.

"He didn't want me—"

"What?"

"I was too threatening, I suppose. I was earning more money than he was and my career was more glamorous." She started stacking the plates nervously. "It was more than he could handle."

"Wasn't he proud of you?"

Kirsten sighed and shook her head. "I don't think so. Anyway, it didn't work out and he and I are both happier."

"And he's remarried."

"Yes, look, I'd rather not talk about it, okay?"

"Why not? Do you still care for him?"

She looked at the ceiling before letting her eyes settle on him. "I don't love him and I sometimes wonder if I ever did. But I don't feel comfortable talking about the divorce." She settled back in her chair. "I guess it all stems from the fact that I really don't believe in divorce. Once you're married, I think it's your responsibility to stick it out."

"But you couldn't—"

"Because he didn't want to. It seemed foolish to continue to live a lie and both be miserable." Her cheeks had colored and she was forced to look away from the honesty in his eyes.

"I didn't mean to pry," he said, setting his coffee cup on the table.

Her smile was frail. "You didn't. It's just not a subject that I'm particularly fond of."

"Then there's no reason to discuss it—unless that miserable son of a bitch ever comes near you again."

"I don't think you have to worry much about that. The last I heard, he and his wife were living in Alaska."

"Too bad it's not Australia."

Kirsten had to laugh. "I love you, counselor."

Dane's lips pulled into an amused smile and he rose from the table. "And I love you, Ms. McQueen. Now, if we could only find a way to deal with this petty little lawsuit you insist on holding over Harmon Smith's head, we'd be able to sort out our differences."

"I doubt it," she murmured playfully, her green eyes lighting with a seductive spark.

His brows rose in interest. "You're challenging me, and if you don't watch out, I'll be forced to . . ."

"What? Tar and feather me? Draw and quarter me?"

White teeth flashed against dark skin. "I've got a better idea," he suggested, pulling her out of her chair and pressing the length of his body against hers.

"I know—you'd rather bore me to death by reading to me from law journals."

His eyes grew dark. "You might be right. There was this case . . ." His hands pressed firmly against the small of her back, rubbing circles of desire against her flesh. "I think it was the notorious Ferguson versus McQueen decision, where the woman taunted the man into making love to her for a solid forty-eight hours . . ." His lips touched hers in a possessive kiss that warmed the womanly fires of desire smoldering deep within the most private part of her.

Her hands wound around his neck and her fingers twined in the dark strands of his hair. Her lips returned the ardor of his kiss and her tongue moved against the smooth polish of his teeth. "Guilty as charged, counselor," she said. Her body pressed urgently against his and he groaned in frustration.

"How am I ever going to leave you?" he whispered, holding her desperately.

"Don't, love. Stay with me," she murmured.

"Kirsten, I can't." But his hands reached upward to cup a straining breast. When he touched the taut nipple he surrendered to the desire burning in his veins. Slowly he eased her body to the floor. "I must be out of my mind . . ."

Chapter Fourteen

$\mathcal{D}$ane hadn't returned to Oregon. Though he had called Kirsten several times, the telephone conversations had been cold and impersonal. Kirsten sensed that he still cared for her, but as the court date approached, the unspoken tension over the wires made her uncomfortable. The lawsuit became an ever-widening abyss that separated them, and Kirsten chided herself for loving a man who would, no doubt, try his best to destroy her reputation.

She had tried to concentrate on anything other than the impending court date, but it had been impossible to get interested in the various articles she was researching and writing.

The first serious job opportunity since she was fired from KPSC had presented itself, and Kirsten had interviewed with the station manager of a small San Francisco television station. He had been a friendly sort, though reserved, and Kirsten hoped to land the job. The position wasn't available until October, though, and Kirsten couldn't help but wonder if negative publicity over the lawsuit would kill her chances of getting it. What station manager in his right mind would hire a reporter with a track record of suing the station that employed her?

Time passed slowly. The weekend before the trial was scheduled Kirsten did anything to keep her mind off the forthcoming battle in the courtroom. She had already packed a suitcase, as she planned to stay in Portland during the trial, and she managed to find miscellaneous tasks to keep her busy.

She was now running five miles every morning and had managed to paint the cabin when she had too much nervous energy to work on her free-lance assignments. Her appetite had fallen off sharply, but she realized that until the trial was over, she wouldn't have much interest in food, or anything else for that matter. The thought of seeing Dane from the opposite side of the courtroom tied her insides in uncomfortable knots and she shuddered to think what he could do if he really was a character assassin.

She was staring blankly down at the typewriter, her fingers poised hesitantly over the keys, when she heard a car door slam. Her painful daydreams were instantly shattered and her heart leaped to her throat as she thought for a wild, expectant moment that it might be Dane. She reasoned that sooner or later he'd have to come to Portland to try the case, though that didn't necessarily mean that he would jeopardize his position by risking a visit to her. But she couldn't help the hope from welling in her heart.

She had already gotten out of the chair and had

reached the opposite side of the room when the visitor knocked. Kirsten opened the door with shaking hands.

Dane was standing on the porch. Kirsten found it difficult to swallow as the emotions of relief and quiet despair clogged her throat.

"Come in," she whispered, her small smile quaking.

"I shouldn't be here," he admitted, but accepted her quiet invitation and entered the familiar cabin with its lofty view of the sea.

Dane's tanned skin was stretched tightly over his cheekbones, and though he was dressed casually in gray cords and a lightweight cotton shirt, he seemed different from the last time she had seen him. He'd changed somehow, taken on a more aloof and sophisticated air. His eyes were more intense, his jawline stronger and even his slight Eastern accent seemed more pronounced.

"Then why did you come?" she asked warily. *Dear God*, she thought, *he's going to tell me it's over and then he's going to go about his business of crucifying me in the courtroom.* She steadied herself against the door as she closed it.

When she had effectively shut out the rest of the world, his eyes, now flecked with gold, silently embraced hers and destroyed all her fears.

"Because I had to." He stared into her worried gaze and then let out a disgusted breath of air. Slowly he placed his arms around her waist and put his forehead against her hair. "I've missed you, Kirsten," he said. His voice was ragged with the emotions ripping him apart. "I had to see you again—it's been so long . . . so very long." His lips brushed her hair and Kirsten felt as if her knees would give way. The sting of wistful tears threatened her eyes.

"I know, love," she whispered hoarsely, feeling the warmth of his hands press against her back. She stood against him, matching each of his strong muscles with smaller counterparts. She could hear the irregular pounding of his heart and feel his ragged breath as it whispered through her hair. Possessively his arms held her and she thought she would cry with joy at his familiar touch. How long had she waited for this moment, wondered if he would ever again claim her body with his?

His lips touched hers and his hands moved upward, softly feeling the pulse jumping near her throat. She closed her eyes and gave in to the powerful feelings of love running through her veins like liquid fire.

When his hand slipped under the hem of her blouse to cup a breast, she gasped in anticipation. His tongue took advantage of the moment and slid past her teeth to flick against the deepest corners of her mouth. "I've wanted you so badly," he groaned when their lips parted and he lifted his head to look once again in the velvet-soft depths of her eyes.

Lovingly, he brushed a strand of honey-brown hair off her face and noticed the unbidden tears welling in the corners of her eyes.

"I've never intended to hurt you," he whispered before gently kissing a quiet tear as it ran down her cheek. Kirsten felt as if her heart would break with his earnest words of love.

"I love you, Dane—it doesn't matter."

"But it does, damn it," he thought aloud. "That's the whole point. If things were different . . ." His voice trailed off, the words lost in the still afternoon air.

"What?"

"If things were different, I'd ask you to marry me, Kirsten, and I wouldn't take no for an answer."

"If things were different," she repeated, her voice catching. But nothing had changed. They were still worlds apart, held together by a thin cord of physical attraction and the vague promise of love. "Look, Dane, I don't think we should be discussing hypothetical situations—" She tried to pull away from him and think rationally. She had to ignore the magic of his words, avoid contact with his sensual hands.

"I just want you to know how I feel."

"Let's not talk about it. Everything is just going to get more confusing and contradictory," she whispered, her heart wrenching painfully.

Shaking his dark head, he frowned. "I couldn't let you come into that courtroom without seeing you beforehand."

"I—I appreciate that. And I love you for it. But I think that us, being together, right before we go to court, will only confuse me and the issues . . . unless that's what you want."

His head snapped upward and he looked as if he'd been struck. His hazel eyes impaled her with needle-sharp honesty. "I came only because I love you, Kirsten, and I want you to know that regardless of what happens on Wednesday, I care for you."

Closing her eyes and squeezing back the tears, she shook her head and held up her palms as if in surrender. "We can't discuss this, Dane. It's too dangerous. It just won't work."

Suddenly his arms were around her and this time the embrace was fierce and demanding. He studied the doubt in her eyes. "I love you, Kirsten, and I want you to know it. Nothing, I repeat, nothing that happens in court will change that."

"Oh, God, Dane, I want to believe you."

"Then just try! For once don't try to reason everything out; trust your instincts!" When his lips found hers, the passion of six long weeks erupted. No longer was he careful or gentle. His hands were warm, possessive and demanding as they quickly removed her clothes and touched the most sensitive parts of her body in familiar caresses that made her breathing shallow.

His own desire was burning in his loins, aching to be relieved by the only woman he had let touch his mind as well as his body. Urgently, he pushed her to the floor, and she felt the weight of his torso crush against her breasts.

The warmth of his hands soothed her, quieted her fears and she was caught up in the furious storm of desire that only he could inspire. She felt his long legs through his trousers as they rubbed insistently against hers. His tongue touched her, tasted her and caused shivering sensations to filter through the whole of her being.

Her fingers deftly removed his clothes and then lingered to feel the rippling movements of his muscles. Desire, like a caged bird suddenly released, soared upward through her body, and her lips returned the fever of his kiss with each ragged breath she took.

"Make love to me," he urged, rolling on his back and placing her above him. The desire in his eyes coupled with the lines of worry on his face made it impossible for her to deny his bold request. His fingers touched each dark-tipped breast as she slowly molded herself to the strong contours of his body.

She felt his sweat mingling with hers, tasted the salt of it on her tongue when she kissed his neck. He groaned and propelled himself upward, his arms encircling her and his hands pressing firmly on her buttocks.

"Please," he cried, his eyes shutting as if in agony. "Kirsten . . ." Slowly she moved over him, positioning herself to accept the promise of his love. His neck strained as she lowered herself on him and began moving in the gentle rhythm of lovemaking.

Her warmth spread over him, heating his blood until it became white hot and pulsed violently in his eardrums. It rushed through him, increasing the pressure and the ache in his loins. He accepted her gentle rhythm and then began to move with her, increasing the heated tempo until Kirsten thought she would explode with the molten fires burning within her.

He stiffened and a shock wave passed from his body through hers, shattering her existence into fragments of sparkling light that touched her soul and blended with the universe.

"I love you," he whispered as the weight of her body rested against him and her breasts flattened over his chest. His fingers idly curled an errant lock of her hair. "I love you more than I thought it was possible to care for one woman."

"Then why, Dane?" she asked quietly. "Why must you defend the station?"

"I don't have any choice in the matter, Kirsten—not like you do."

"It's your job." The defeat in her voice made her sound weary.

"More than that. I explained it to you before." His hand tenderly touched the gentle slope of her spine.

"When this is all over, my lady, we have a few things to discuss," he promised.

"Such as?"

"Such as how I'm going to convince you to marry me."

She pulled away from him, just far enough to gaze into his eyes. "Are you serious?" she asked skeptically. But she couldn't contain the small smile that curved her lips.

"More serious than I've ever been in my life." He propped up on one elbow and stared into the mysterious depths of her eyes. "And if I can, I'm going to try to straighten out this mess of a lawsuit." He reached for his cords, jerked them over his legs and buckled his belt.

Kirsten had managed to get into her jeans and was buttoning her blouse. "And how do you propose to do that, counselor?"

"I've been working on the Ginevra story."

"And?" she prodded him. Her heart was pounding frantically in her chest. Maybe there was still a glimmer of hope that they could find a way to be together, not as opponents in a court battle, but as one man and one woman.

He shrugged his tense shoulders. "And nothing, at least not yet. I feel that I'm close, but . . . ."

"You're running out of time," she finished for him.

He nodded curtly, stood and paced between the window and the fireplace. "What about you?"

"Not much better, I'm afraid," she admitted. "I went to see that woman who heads up the fight against nuclear power, what was her name, the friend of the reporter at *The Herald* . . . June Dellany, that was it. She was very supportive, but she couldn't give me any information that would help."

Kirsten stood and ran her fingers through the tangles in her hair. "Even if I knew anything more, I don't know that it would help—especially not now. The trial starts Wednesday."

The conversation had become so intense that neither Dane nor Kirsten had heard the sound of a car as it ground to a halt in the gravel near the garage. It was only after the car door slammed and footsteps echoed on the front porch that Kirsten became aware of the visitor.

Dane's sharp eyes moved to the doorway and a small muscle in the back of his jaw tightened.

"Oh, dear God," Kirsten murmured as she stepped to answer the door. Dane's hand restrained her.

"I think I should leave."

"How? By the back door?" Kirsten's green eyes registered her indignation and she shook her head while attempting to straighten the tangled golden-brown curls with her fingers. "We have nothing to hide, Dane. It's probably just the paper boy coming to collect."

"You're sure about this?"

"Absolutely." She pulled free of his cautious grasp and jerked open the door.

On the porch, looking slightly perplexed and worried, stood Lloyd Grady. He pondered Kirsten's face for a fleeting moment before looking into the cabin.

"I'm sorry I didn't call," he said half-apologetically, "but something's come up and I can't make our appointment on Monday. I thought we'd better go over a few things today—and if you have any questions, we'll work them out this afternoon or on Tuesday, whichever is better for you . . ." His voice faded as he met the curious eyes of the man he was to oppose in the courtroom.

Lloyd's tanned face drained of all color. "What the hell?" After reconfirming what he had hoped was just a figment of his imagination, his furious gaze returned to his client. "What's going on here?" he asked in a clipped voice.

"Why don't you come in?" Kirsten suggested, her fluttering heart refusing to calm.

Lloyd placed his hands on his hips, pushing aside his suit jacket. "Wait a minute . . ."

"I think you'd better come in, Grady," Dane said, reinforcing Kirsten's offer. "Maybe we can talk this out."

"Look, Ferguson, I don't know what's going on here . . ." His pained eyes searched Kirsten's face. "I'm not sure I want to know, but I think we can forget about discussing it. The fact that you're here is not only unethical, it's—"

"It's my right," Dane finished for him. "Kirsten and I are friends."

"Friends!" Lloyd thundered, shaking his hands in the air. "If you're her friend, then you can't very well call yourself objective in this matter, can you? I think you owe it to Harmon Smith and Fletcher Ross to remove yourself from the case!"

"I can't do that."

"But you're the defending attorney, for God's sake!" Lloyd was shaking and red in the face, but something in the deadly glare in Dane's eyes made him pull himself together. The last thing he could afford was to let Dane Ferguson rattle him—in the courtroom or out of it. Nervously he tugged at one end of his blond moustache.

"Maybe we should be talking settlement," Dane ventured, moving out of the doorway and allowing Lloyd to pass.

"Not on your life, Ferguson. I've been working on this case day and night, and I'm not about to let it go."

"Don't you think you should consult your client?" Dane asked, cocking his head in Kirsten's direction.

Lloyd confronted Kirsten with a look that could kill. "I don't understand you, Kirsten," he said, his voice still shaking. "We've worked hard, won that first trial, and now you throw it all away on an affair with him? What the devil's gotten into you? Can't you tell your friends from your enemies?"

"I don't think you understand," Kirsten said.

"You bet I don't!" Despite his efforts to the contrary, Lloyd lost his cool. His fist crashed into the wall. "Kirsten, why didn't you tell me? If you wanted out of the suit, all you had to do was call!" He shook his head, his outrage evident in the scowl of frustration contorting his even features. "How could you have been so stupid?"

"I think that's enough," Dane interjected firmly.

"Excuse me, Ferguson," Lloyd lashed back. "I'm having a discussion with my client."

"Then quit yelling at me, Lloyd," Kirsten replied. "Treat me like your client instead of your wife."

Lloyd reacted as if Kirsten had struck him. After a moment's shock he began to speak, and his voice was considerably lower than it had been. He tossed an insolent thumb in Dane's direction, and his blond brows rose quizzically. "Didn't I tell you about him? Didn't I warn you that he would do anything to win this suit?"

"Wait a minute—" Dane cut in, striding over to Lloyd and staring at him with contempt.

Lloyd ignored him. "The trial is less than a week away, Kirsten. What the devil are you trying to do—sabotage the whole goddamn suit?"

"I think you should leave," Dane stated firmly. An angry muscle was working in the corner of his jaw and his thumb was rubbing threateningly against his forefinger. The look in his eyes suggested that he would just as soon strangle Lloyd as confront him in the courtroom.

"I should leave? I was just going to suggest that you take a hike!"

"Stop it!" Kirsten's voice rose above the rage sparking between the two men. "Can't we talk this over like adults?"

"Sound advice," Dane agreed. "I still think a settlement is the best option for both parties."

"Not on your life."

"Lloyd, why not?" Kirsten asked. A settlement. It would solve all of her problems. No confrontation in the courtroom, and it would almost be like winning against Aaron Becker, Harmon Smith and the rest of the lot.

"Because we've got them running scared, that's why not!" Lloyd said, a sly smile pulling at the corners of his mouth. "Otherwise he would never have suggested it."

"I don't care, Lloyd. I'm tired, and I don't honestly know if I can go through another court battle. This way, the press will get wind of it, and it will seem as if I've won." Kirsten's eyes roved between the tense faces of the two men, one she loved as passionately as life itself, the other she had trusted most of her thirty-five years.

"I'll have to advise you against it." Lloyd's face was set in firm resolve. Kirsten knew he doubted that she would ever question his judgment.

A weary sigh escaped her. A settlement would represent an end to the fighting and a chance to be with Dane. It would also end any chance for the rumor of her affair with Dane to be made public. A scandal right now would be disastrous to her case and his reputation. "I want to settle," she said firmly.

Lloyd's lips compressed into a thin, tight line. "If it's what you want."

"It is, Lloyd. It's time for me to get back on my feet again and leave the lawsuit and KPSC behind me."

For the first time since setting eyes on Lloyd Grady, Dane smiled. "I'll call Aaron Becker and Harmon Smith."

Relief, like a cool wave, washed over Kirsten. "You can use the phone in the bedroom." Dane walked through the living room, down the short hallway and into the bedroom before closing the door softly behind him. Kirsten offered Lloyd a sincere smile and took Lloyd's arm. "Come on, let me buy you a cup of coffee."

When they were seated at the kitchen table, Lloyd took a long sip of his coffee and rotated the cup nervously in his hands. "You could have told me, you know," he said after an uncomfortable silence.

She shook her head and frowned. "No, I couldn't have. You threatened to walk off the case—"

"But I never imagined you were . . . involved with the man. Damn it, Kirsten, you should have told me."

"It's all working out for the best anyway," she said, avoiding the unnamed accusation in his eyes.

At the sound of Dane's approaching footsteps Kirsten turned to smile and face the man she loved. The look of defeat on his face when he entered the room shattered all her dreams as surely as if they were fine porcelain.

"Harmon Smith refuses to settle," Dane announced, leaning against the doorjamb.

"Maybe that's because his attorney advised him against it," Lloyd surmised with a triumphant gleam in his eye. He set his unfinished cup on the table. "So it looks like we'll meet in court after all."

Dane's dark brows rose. "That's about the size of it—unless your client wants to drop the case."

"No way," Kirsten replied, her lips tightening and her eyes cold. The thought of Smith forcing the issue made her blood boil. "If it's a fight Harmon Smith wants, it's a fight he'll get."

"Well, this sheds a new light on everything, doesn't it?" Lloyd asked sarcastically. A grim smile spread slowly over his features as he turned his attention to Dane. "Mr. Ferguson, I suggest that the next time you want to see my client, you tell me about it first."

"Forget it, Grady. The lady makes her own decisions."

"Then use your head, Kirsten," Lloyd warned. "Think about whose side he's on." He cast a knowing look in Kirsten's direction before standing and straightening the cuff of his shirt. "I'll call you later, when we can discuss your side of the issue without the presence of the defense in the room."

Lloyd nodded a quick good-bye to Kirsten and brushed past Dane on his way to the door. When the front door slammed shut and the sound of Lloyd's car engine faded into the distance, Dane turned to Kirsten. "I'm sorry this didn't work out."

"Are you?"

"You know I am." He stared at her for a moment, as if memorizing the soft planes of her face. "Harmon wouldn't hear of a settlement. I really did try to convince him that it was in his own best interest, but he didn't buy it. He insisted that I help Fletcher Ross 'deal with you once and for all.'"

"And you owe him this incredible favor, right?"

"He did manage to bring that up."

"Nice guy," Kirsten murmured as she began picking up the dishes, and consciously avoided Dane's intuitive gaze. She had begun walking to the sink, but paused when he called her name.

"Kirsten, I—"

Turning to meet the questions in his eyes, she shook her head vigorously. The golden rays of the late afternoon sun poured through the window and highlighted the brown strands with streaks of gold. "I know," she whispered, reading his mind. "I think you should leave."

"When this is all over—"

"Shhh. Don't even talk about it." Her smile was wistful. "You'd better go."

The frustration building within him was evident in the strained contours of his rugged face. His knowing eyes held hers for a silent moment, and then he left without saying good-bye.

When she saw Dane's car race down the long drive, Kirsten crumpled into a corner and let her quiet tears of despair run freely down her face.

The courtroom was nearly filled by the time Kirsten took her seat. Newspaper reporters were hastily scribbling notes inside the room while camera crews from local stations were planted firmly outside the courtroom doors. Kirsten recognized several workers from KPSC, who would no doubt be called upon to testify on behalf of the station.

Lloyd was as reassuring as ever, though even he, in his impeccable brown suit, seemed nervous.

Kirsten hadn't slept more than two hours at a stretch from the time Dane had left the beach cabin.

Every time the phone had rung, her heart had raced expectantly, and she had always been disappointed.

Dane hadn't called.

Nor had he come by to check on her.

The battle lines were drawn and the war was about to begin.

Lloyd was opening his briefcase when Dane strode into the courtroom. Even Kirsten was unnerved by his presence. She had warned herself that he would be formidable, but she hadn't expected that his self-assured stature and near arrogant pride in his eyes would be so noticeable. He looked as if he had already won the battle as he walked to his table on the opposite side of the room.

As she looked more closely, she noticed the lines of strain near the corners of his eyes. Though disguised by his East Coast sophistication and charm, the shadowed weariness was evident to her. Kirsten's heart went out to him.

Lloyd noticed the difference in her composure. "Don't forget why he's here, Kirsten," Lloyd warned her. "That smile isn't because he's seen you."

Maybe Lloyd was right. The triumphant smile on Dane's face might well be because he had found a way to completely discredit her, and she wondered fleetingly if he would use his affair with her to show how low she would stoop in her efforts to fight KPSC. In her heart she couldn't believe that he would use her, but he hadn't bothered to call since that last ugly scene with Lloyd at the cabin.

After setting his briefcase on the table, Dane advanced on Kirsten.

"Wait a minute, Ferguson. What's going on?" Lloyd asked, intervening on Kirsten's behalf when Dane was in earshot.

"I want to talk to Kirsten."

"You can't do that. Not here—not now," Lloyd argued, his feathers of protocol ruffled.

Dane's eyes drove into Kirsten's and she read the honesty in his gaze. "It's all right, Lloyd. I'll talk to him."

Begrudgingly Lloyd watched Dane take Kirsten's arm and maneuver her to a quiet corner of the courtroom.

"I've been busy," Dane whispered, letting his hand linger on the tailored sleeve of her linen jacket.

"I imagine—"

"As the lawyer for the defense, I had access to all the records at KPSC. Not just personnel records, but other documents as well."

"So?"

"It took a couple of days, but after poring over everything that the station had to do with Ginevra, I still felt that something was missing. I did some checking. The land for the proposed site is owned by a holding company."

Kirsten nodded. The company was obscure.

"Well, I dug a little deeper. The principal investors of that holding company are none other than our own illustrious Aaron Becker and Harmon Smith. Fletcher Ross knew all about it. I wouldn't be surprised if he was in on the ground floor as well."

"What?"

Dane smiled, and a glimmer of hope entered Kirsten's heart. "From what I can piece together, not only have Becker and Smith speculated and purchased the Ginevra land with the intent to sell it at an astronomical profit, they have also invested in the construction company that is most likely to bid and get the Ginevra job. When you became overly interested in the site, they got nervous and thought you might stumble onto their plans and expose them. The scandal would have ruined KPSC's reputation—or at the very least cost Aaron Becker and Harmon Smith their jobs once the board of directors got wind of it."

Kirsten shook her head at the deception. "So what does this mean?"

"I already talked to Smith. He's agreed to settle out of court with you. Though he hasn't really done anything illegal, he wants to avoid the embarrassment of any bad publicity and he feels that a quiet settlement would be in the interest of all parties concerned. He's agreed to pay all of the original award of two hundred thousand dollars."

Kirsten felt herself begin to stagger, but Dane's arm braced her until her knees became firm once again. "It's not the money, Dane, it never has been."

"You'd rather fight this thing?"

"What do you suggest—not as an attorney for the defense, but . . . as my friend."

His crooked smile broadened engagingly. "I'd say take the money and run."

"But what about the attempted fraud?" Kirsten asked in a tense whisper. "I can't let them get away with that!"

"I think fraud is too strong a term, but I wouldn't worry about it if I were you. When I was talking to Aaron Becker at KPSC, someone overheard part of the conversation. The way news travels in the land of television, you can bet that by the end of the day, it will be given national attention."

Kirsten smiled into Dane's intriguing eyes. "Counselor," she stated, "you've got yourself a deal. Just straighten out the facts and figures with my attorney."

Lloyd took the news in stride and seemed slightly

relieved that he didn't have to battle the New York attorney. In his opinion the settlement was more of a win than a draw and a damn sight better than a loss. Any way you looked at it, it was a feather in his cap.

After the two attorneys advised the court that the case had been settled, Dane took Kirsten's hand and led her out of the courtroom. When Dane pushed the doors open and Kirsten stepped into the hallway, television cameras followed her and several microphones were thrust into her face.

"Ms. McQueen, can you give us any information on the settlement?" one reporter asked. Before Kirsten could respond, another question was put to her.

"Ms. McQueen, is it true that someone at KPSC was involved in the Ginevra scandal?"

"Ms. McQueen, do you consider the settlement a win and would you call it a victory for women workers?"

Kirsten had been walking away from the crowd, but turned gracefully on her heel and stared comfortably into the television cameras. "I'd just like to say that I'm very satisfied with the settlement and that I'd have to thank both the attorneys for the prosecution and the defense for helping to achieve it. Thank you."

"But Ms. McQueen? What about the defending attorney?"

"Mr. Ferguson? Wait a minute, he's the guy on the other side, isn't he? Mr. Ferguson! Could you give us a statement from KPSC?"

Dane shook his head and waved the cameramen away.

Kirsten hurried down the courthouse steps, not feeling the cool drops of rain pouring from the overcast Portland skies. It was over. She was with Dane and nothing else in the world mattered. Not the reporters, not the rain, not even Harmon Smith and Aaron Becker.

Dane helped her into his car and slid behind the wheel. In a matter of minutes they were driving west, leaving the city of Portland, the shimmering Willamette River, and the throng of reporters behind.

"That was rude, you know," Kirsten admonished Dane, snuggling against him.

"What?"

"Ignoring all those questions."

"You think so because you're a reporter." He squinted at the road ahead and placed his hand on her knee. "Have I ever told you what I think of television people?"

"Spare me," she said with a laugh. "By the way, where are you taking me?"

"Home."

"Home?"

He lifted his hand from her knee and draped a possessive arm across her shoulders. "I've mentioned that I'd been busy?"

"Um-hum."

"Well, you see, one of the partners in the firm, he's been interested in buying me out for a long time . . . we finally agreed on a price."

Kirsten's heart missed a beat. "I don't understand."

"Only because you're not really trying. What's happening here, Ms. McQueen, is that I'm proposing to you. I knew that you wouldn't move to New York, and it's too far to commute, so I decided that I'd move to Portland and start a practice here. You don't think Fletcher Ross or Lloyd Grady would mind, do you?"

Kirsten smiled at the thought. "I doubt that they'll be pleased."

"How about you? I think you could use a new attorney as well as a husband. We could live in the city and keep the beach house for vacations—with the children. What do you say? Will you marry me, Kirsten?"

Tears of happiness welled in Kirsten's round eyes. Marriage to Dane and bearing his children were more than she could wish for. "I thought you'd never ask," she whispered throatily.

Dane laughed in contentment. "Let's go home."

Kirsten kissed his cheek and wrapped her arms around him. "Anything you want, counselor."

READERS' COMMENTS ON SILHOUETTE SPECIAL EDITIONS:

"I just finished reading the first six Silhouette Special Edition Books and I had to take the opportunity to write you and tell you how much I enjoyed them. I enjoyed all the authors in this series. Best wishes on your Silhouette Special Editions line and many thanks."

—B.H.*, Jackson, OH

"The Special Editions are really special and I enjoyed them very much! I am looking forward to next month's books."

—R.M.W.*, Melbourne, FL

"I've just finished reading four of your first six Special Editions and I enjoyed them very much. I like the more sensual detail and longer stories. I will look forward each month to your new Special Editions."

—L.S.*, Visalia, CA

"Silhouette Special Editions are. — 1.) Superb! 2.) Great! 3.) Delicious! 4.) Fantastic! . . . Did I leave anything out? These are books that an adult woman can read . . . I love them!"

—H.C.*, Monterey Park, CA

*names available on request

Silhouette Special Edition. Romances for the woman who expects a little more out of love.

If you enjoyed this book, and you're ready for more great romance

...get 4 romance novels FREE when you become a Silhouette Special Edition home subscriber.

Act now and we'll send you four exciting Silhouette Special Edition romance novels. They're our gift to introduce you to our convenient home subscription service. Every month, we'll send you six new passion-filled Special Edition books. Look them over for 15 days. If you keep them, pay just $11.70 for all six. Or return them at no charge.

We'll mail your books to you two full months *before they are available anywhere else.* Plus, with every shipment, you'll receive the Silhouette Books Newsletter absolutely free. *And with Silhouette Special Edition there are never any shipping or handling charges.*

Mail the coupon today to get your four free books—and more romance than you ever bargained for.

Silhouette Special Edition is a service mark and a registered trademark.

MAIL THIS COUPON
and get 4 thrilling

Silhouette Desire®

novels **FREE** (a $7.80 value)

Silhouette Desire books may not be for everyone. They *are* for readers who want a sensual, provocative romance. These are modern love stories that are charged with emotion from the first page to the thrilling happy ending—about women who discover the extremes of fiery passion. Confident women who face the challenge of today's world and overcome all obstacles to attain their dreams—*and their desires.*

We believe you'll be so delighted with Silhouette Desire romance novels that you'll want to receive them regularly through our home subscription service. Your books will be *shipped to you two months before they're available anywhere else*—so you'll never miss a new title. Each month we'll send you 6 new books to look over for 15 days, without obligation. If not delighted, simply return them and owe nothing. Or keep them and pay only $1.95 each. There's no charge for postage or handling. And there's no obligation to buy anything at any time. You'll also receive a subscription to the Silhouette Books Newsletter *absolutely free!*

So don't wait. To receive your four FREE books, fill out and mail the coupon below *today!*

SILHOUETTE DESIRE and colophon are registered trademarks and a service mark.